D1607780

MULTIPLE-OPTION MARCHING BAND TECHNIQUES

A Foster

SECOND EDITION

Newly edited and revised. Includes
additional and expanded
Drills and a complete
Corps Chapter.

Copyright © 1975 and 1978 Alfred Publishing Company, Inc.

All Rights Reserved.
No part of this book may be reproduced
or transmitted in any form
or by any means, electronic or mechanical
including photocopying or recording
without permission in writing from the publisher.

Library of Congress Cataloging in Publication Data

Foster, Robert E.
Multiple option, marching band techniques.

1. Marching bands. I. Title. II. Title:
Marching band techniques.

MT733.F68   785'.06'7108   75-4595
ISBN 0-88284-066-5

Second Edition

CONTENTS

CONTENTS continued

DIAGRAM AND DRILL CHART LISTING

DIAGRAM AND DRILL CHART LISTING continued

Block Band Drills

Preface

Many teachers dislike the fall marching band season because they have never had an opportunity to learn to teach effectively in this performance area; many have never experienced the excitement and pleasure of producing a fine, truly exciting halftime performance. The satisfaction one derives from succeeding in this area is no less real than the satisfaction one enjoys in presenting a thrilling concert. Perhaps the most obvious difference in these two performance situations is that the concert is most likely to reach an audience of 500 to 1,000 persons, while the marching performance may be enjoyed by an audience of 5,000 or 50,000, or one million, depending on your location, your school, and the radio and television coverage.

MULTIPLE OPTION MARCHING TECHNIQUES are not original concepts. They represent an amalgamation and blending of nearly half a century of progress and innovations in marching techniques and drill devices. The beauty and strength of this plan lie in its complete flexibility. By using the basic rules, principles, and fundamentals explained herein, any band can take advantage of the last several decades.

This is, therefore, a "HOW TO" book for the high school or college band director, with a little bit of "WHY" thrown in.

To the author's knowledge this is the first book of its kind which attempts to explain the historical development of the marching band from earliest times to the present. It is felt that this background provides a depth of understanding which helps place the marching band in its proper perspective as related to other performing organizations.

Preface

The author is especially indebted to all those dedicated teachers who have contributed to the progress of the marching band, and who continue to contribute to the artistic and entertainment growth of this performance medium.

I am especially indebted to those teachers whose love, dedication, concern, and skill with the band have contributed so greatly to my own personal life: Estill Foster, my father, and band director for ten of the most important years of my life; Vincent R. DiNino, director of the University of Texas Longhorn Band, my college band director; and Richard W. Bowles, Director of Bands, University of Florida, my friend and colleague the first seven years of my college teaching career.

Robert E. Foster

1
A Short History of the Marching Band

Marching bands have a great heritage! While there are those defending or attacking today's marching band, it is unfortunate that we tend to ignore the historical facts which indicate the marching band was among the very first ensembles of wind, string, and/or percussion instruments developed in our earliest civilizations. We frequently tend to ignore our heritage.

The history of the marching band reveals itself to be much more than merely a history of men walking around playing wind instruments. Actually, in its early stages it is a chronicle of instrumental music. The earliest marching bands were, indeed, the forerunners of today's symphony orchestras, concert bands, and instrumental chamber music, as well as the modern marching band. The historical development of the marching band, therefore, cannot be separated from that of the concert band, or the other instrumental performing groups found today.

The progress and development of instrumental music in the various periods of history were dependent on both the social and the political climate of the times. They were also nearly always closely linked to three types, or groups of people:

1. *Performers* and *patrons*—those actually producing the music; or those who encouraged or made possible the performances, including conductors.
2. *Composers*—those who created the music to be performed.
3. *Musical instrument makers*—those inventors, performers, or conductors who contributed to the technical development and improvement in the instruments themselves, thus making further tonal and technical resources available to both composers and performers.

In this book we shall identify and credit some of those outstanding personalities whose contributions have been most important in the development of wind and percussion musical performances from the earliest times to the present.

From Ancient Times through the Fifteenth Century

Ancient Times

In the days of the Old Testament, processions took place to the accompaniment of various kinds of martial music, at times using early forms of trumpets which are mentioned frequently in the Bible. It is possible that the Hebrews learned about the trumpet while they were captives of the Egyptians. According to Hebrew historians, the trumpet became very popular and by the time of King Solomon there were reputed to be 200,000 trumpets in use. These instruments were 21 inches long and were made of metal. Although they were used primarily in worship services, they were also used on the field of battle. These are the same kind of trumpets that Joshua is said to have used in the battle of Jericho, where the walls of the city crumbled and fell as the trumpeters played and marched around them.

There are historical references to the martial music of the Egyptians, Assyrians, Greeks, and Romans, as well as the Hebrews, which indicate that they all used instruments similar to our timpani, hand drums, cymbals, and tambourines.

The ancient Greeks had six types of trumpets or horns. Best known of these was the salpinx, which was used by them during the siege of Troy. Trumpet playing became a very popular art with the Greeks, and trumpet playing contests were added to their olympic games.

2

It is also known that the Greeks used a kind of rhythmic procession with musical accompaniment for the entrances and exits in their tragedies. These may well be the first known marching "performances," as contrasted with utilitarian marching, or the movement of troops.

We know that the Roman armies marched to the rhythmic pulse of military type music. One of the earliest military bands was formed by Servius Tullius (570 B.C.) who introduced the bronze trumpet into the Roman army. Three types of military trumpets and horns were developed by the Romans: the cornu, the lituus, and the tuba. When Rome was finally conquered, the victorious Europeans presumably carried examples of Roman trumpets back to their homes introducing these instruments to that part of the world.

Lituus (Roman trumpet). An instrument in the Vatican Museum at Rome.

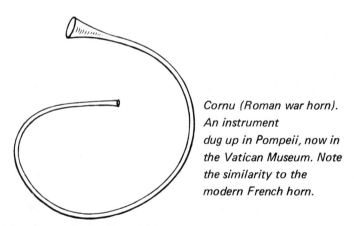

Cornu (Roman war horn).
An instrument
dug up in Pompeii, now in
the Vatican Museum. Note
the similarity to the
modern French horn.

Christianity through the Crusades

About the time of the beginnings of Christianity, war songs or chants were sung or shouted by men marching at the head of troops on the way to do battle. Their original purpose is supposed to have been to inspire their men as they marched. Gradually the chants became more rhythmic, finally becoming songs with added words.

3

During the reign of Charlemagne there were numerous song-chants which described various battles and individual accomplishments.

In the eleventh century, trumpets had become very popular with military groups because of their carrying power and portability. They became the private domain of the nobility who made up the cavalry units, while the fife, bagpipe, and drums became associated with foot soldiers.

Before the twelfth century, popular non-military music was performed primarily by wandering minstrels, and it was through these minnesingers and meistersingers that many of the ancient songs were spread throughout Europe.

The banding together of these musicians was at that time simply a matter of momentary convenience, and their concerted efforts were limited to playing songs, dance tunes, and marches. These minstrels were strictly forbidden to use trumpets or drums as these instruments were restricted to the exclusive use of princes and noblemen. Both trumpets and kettle-drums were used in the bands which performed for ceremonial occasions at the courts of the kings and queens of England.

In the thirteenth century, a number of European musicians who had established themselves in towns became dissatisfied with having their status classified along with the wandering minstrels. They therefore joined together for mutual protection and formed organizations which were called guilds.

The first guild was formed in Vienna in 1288, and eventually guilds of this type were created in most of the larger towns of Europe. Later, these towns prohibited wandering musicians from playing within their boundaries and formed regular bands of their own to provide music for local needs. Thus the first seeds of our modern bands were sown in these little groups. They were led by a regular artisan, or Stadtpfeifer, and were comprised of about four performers plus several apprentices. Their instrumentation was usually limited to fifes, flutes, shalmes (a soprano instrument in the oboe family), bombard (a sort of tenor or bass oboe), zinks, bagpipes, viols, and drums. Apparently they played whatever instruments were required for the occasion—strings, woodwinds, or brasses, depending on whether the event was indoors or out; marching, standing, or seated; a civic celebration, a wedding, or a funeral.

A group of musicians (oliphant, one-handed flute with drum, and trumpet) from the engraving, "The Fest of Herodias" by Israel van Meckenem (d.1509).

In 1426 the town of Augsburg was granted the privilege of maintaining a group of town trumpeters and kettle-drummers. This grant came directly from the Emperor, and it was eventually extended to most other free towns, finally enabling European musicians to use trumpets in ordinary public (nonroyal or unofficial) performances.

There is an interesting reference to a combination of fifes and drums which were used with the Swiss Landed Knights' armies in the fifteenth century. They are reported to have played marching tunes and appropriate songs for various occasions in camp (concert), at ceremonial parades (marching shows), or simply with moving soldiers on the march.

Sixteenth and Seventeenth Centuries

The Venetian School and the Age of Splendor

One of the first great composers known to have written for a military band was Andrea Gabrieli (1510–1586), whose *Aria della Battaglia* was performed by oboes, slide trumpets, and trombones.

His nephew, Giovanni Gabrieli (1557–1612) was one of the leading members of the Venetian school, and his work, *Sonata Pian e Forte,* is the first composed work known to have been written for a specifically prescribed instrumentation. The first chorus is for zink or cornetto and three trombones, and the second is for a viola and three trombones, giving us our first example of orchestration.

Throughout the sixteenth and seventeenth centuries music continued to be developed to accompany processions and ceremonies of the guilds and townsmen, and in Germany during this time there developed a great tradition in brass playing. The musicians in these cities were civil servants, and many of these towns, especially in Germany and Austria, began to take great pride in their official or semi-official musical performances. By the time of Bach they were playing chorales from their towers, and providing music for all important civic occasions, festivals, state and academic ceremonies, funerals, and weddings.

Johann Pezel (1639–1694) wrote many pieces for these groups of musicians to use on less sacred occasions. A number of these are in publication today and are still performed by small wind groups.

In his book, *The Wind Band*, Richard Franko Goldman states that "these little bands of tower musicians were in many real senses the precursors of the civilian concert bands we know today. Their functions, if not their instrumentation, were identical . . . It is from these groups that the popular (as opposed to the military) aspect of band music stems. From the military, the town band . . . absorbed the trumpet and drum, just as the military band in turn absorbed the trombone and the instruments which began to emerge in the eighteenth century.

"The (marching) band as we know it today may be said to stem partly from the fifes, drums, and trumpets associated with the European courts and armies, and partly from the ensemble of similar instruments used for secular music in the sixteenth and seventeenth

Three trumpeters, from H. Aldegrever's series,
"The Wedding Dancers," 1583.

centuries. It is the eventual modification and merging of these two usages that resulted in the prototype of the military band."

The French Influence and Lully

The most important bands in France were in the court of Louis XIV, where the musicians were under the leadership of Jean Baptiste Lully (1632–1687). An outstanding musician and well known composer, Lully quickly brought order and discipline to his organizations. He was a prolific composer and is still well known for his many ballets and operas. It is less known, however, that he wrote many marches for his band which survive today as excellent examples of very early music written for band. It is interesting to note that Lully was apparently the first composer to write out his drum parts, being credited as the only composer who attempted drum notation before 1777.

The oboe made its first appearance in France about 1650. Lully's bands had been performing at outdoor ceremonies using the traditional instruments (shawms and bassoons) led by the shawm. However, the emergence of the oboe eventually made the shawm obsolete, contributing to the excellence and position of leadership that Lully's groups enjoyed.

The French bands that Lully led for Louis XIV are the first infantry bands of which we have a reliable record.

Late Seventeenth Century

Bands and guilds continued to flourish. In England in 1680, the Elector of Saxony had in his employ twenty court trumpeters and three kettle-drummers. At about the same time the court trumpeters and drummers in the German Empire formed a new guild through which they enjoyed special privileges and special protection.

Until the seventeenth century, most of the music performed by the bands of trumpeters was passed on from player to player by rote; it was not written down. When royal personages joined their soldiers in the field they were accompanied by their trumpeters. These musicians played both for signalling and for the entertainment of the marchers or campers. Since these musicians served on horse-back, the trumpets became identified with the mounted troops, eventually becoming regularly attached to the cavalry.

About this time the trombone came into more prominent use and was combined with other instruments of that period (flutes, oboes, pommers, zinks or cornetti, and occasionally trumpets and kettle-drums). The sound of these little bands began to improve and they started to more nearly resemble our modern bands.

Bands became distinguished into three distinct classes, each with its own purpose. There were bands for the mounted cavalry; bands for the marching, or foot, soldier; and civilian bands. The full orchestra emerged and concentrated its efforts in the direction of the cultivated musical elite, while bands played for everyone.

Eighteenth and Early Nineteenth Centuries

Development of Band Literature

The most significant composer of music for bands after Lully was Johann Philipp Krieger, who wrote a number of suites for wind instruments in 1704. His bandstration was divided into four parts: 1st treble (oboe), 2nd treble (oboe), taille (the tenor voice—frequently played by an alto oboe), and bass (bassoon). This was a combination of voices that was very common in the English military bands of the day, using as many as three players on the 1st and 4th parts, two on the 2nd, and one on the 3rd. A trumpet was sometimes substituted for the alto oboe. This same combination of voices was used by most of the Prussian military bands existing throughout the eighteenth century.

In 1747 Johann Sebastian Bach (1685–1750) wrote a piece for this instrumentation called *Marche pour la Premiere Garde du Roy*. In England, France, and Austria horns were being used with more frequency, and on some occasions trumpets were added, but always there were still the double reeds.

Johann Christian Bach's (1735–1782) marches were written especially for the Band of the Hanoverian Guards. This eight piece band included two oboes, two clarinets, two horns, and two bassoons. Mozart's *Serenades, K.375* and *K.388,* were written for a band of this instrumentation, while his earlier *Serenade No. 10, K.361,* was scored for two oboes, two clarinets, two basset horns, two bassoons, four horns and double bass. Later in his career, J. C. Bach wrote

9

several Symphonies for Wind Instruments using only quintet and sextet combinations. These were written about 1780 and were so scored that they could also be played by cavalry regiments which had smaller bands. His two marches for the Prince of Wales' Light Dragoons, written for two clarinets, two horns, and one bassoon, also fit this pattern.

In Austria a difference between concert and marching groups evolved: (a) a concert ensemble of six to eight wind instruments was called Harmoniemusik, and (b) the groups that were used with the military were called Feldharmonie. Franz Joseph Haydn (1732–1809), at the age of twenty-nine, entered into the service of the Esterhazy family at Eisenstadt not far from Vienna. During that employ he wrote a number of marches for the Feldharmonie of Prince Esterhazy.

C. P. E. Bach (1714–1788), after spending almost thirty years of his life as a chamber musician to Frederick the Great, became musical director of the six principal churches in Hamburg and one of the most influential musicians of the eighteenth century. During this period he composed several outdoor sonatas for two flutes, two clarinets, two horns, and bassoon. The composer, Dittersdorf, used two oboes, two horns and one bassoon for his *Partitas* which were composed about the same time.

Because of music especially edited for them in 1783, we know the instrumentation of the band of the Coldstream Guards included clarinets, horns, and bassoons. The English military marches written by Franz Joseph Haydn later in his life were for that same combination of instruments; added were a trumpet, a second bassoon, and a serpent. Haydn wrote three of these that are of particular significance: his *March in Eb*, which was probably a march for mounted use; his *March in C*, which is slower and presumably intended for foot soldiers; and his *March for the Prince of Wales*. All of these works are still available for performance by bands today.

In 1796 Michael Haydn, younger brother of Joseph, wrote a Turkish March for a band which included two flutes, two oboes, two clarinets, two horns, two bassoons, two trumpets, bass drum, and cymbals. Thus the growth in the size of ensembles continued.

An instrumentation peak was reached early in the nineteenth century with the grandiose ideas of Hector Berlioz. In addition to providing the world with its first book on orchestation, he expanded the size and scope of the orchestra and band to new dimensions. His *Requiem* is a major work that incorporates a brass band for performance, and his *Grand Symphony for Band, Funeral, and Triumphant* was first performed by a band of 108 players, a string orchestra, and a large chorus.

Richard Wagner wrote his *Trauersinfonie* as a funeral march for the ceremonies in 1844 for the final burial in Dresden of Carl Maria von Weber. Among the other well-known composers who contributed to the wind and band literature are Beethoven, Handel, Mendelssohn, Rossini, Donizetti, and Schubert.

A discussion of band literature cannot conclude without recognizing the significant contributions of the English composers Gustaf Holst (1873–1934) and Ralph Vaughn Williams (1872–1958) who contributed the first significant music for the military band in this century, and the many English band leaders and writers like Kenneth Alford (whose real name was Major Fred Rickets) who have left us with a great legacy of British band music and tradition.

Development of Band Instrumentation

One can hardly discuss the development of bands and band music without mentioning the continuous changes and improvements which occurred in the groups' instrumentation.

Primitive flutes (pipes), stringed instruments, trumpets, and drums have existed since our earliest recorded history. It is the refinement of these old instruments and the invention or development of new ones with which we shall concern ourselves.

We have seen the band grow from the trumpets and drums of medieval times, through the more sophisticated groups of the guilds, and into the eighteenth century. The trumpet finally lost its "reserved" status and was added to the infantry bands and various percussion instruments such as cymbals and triangles also came into use as a result of the popularity of the Turkish Janizary bands. Trombones were finally accepted by military bands near the end of the eighteenth century.

Early in the eighteenth century German military bands were considered superior to all others in Europe. Their basic instrumentation included two flutes, two oboes, two horns, one or two trumpets, two bassoons, and a bass trombone or serpent. Interestingly, their instrumentation did not include percussion.

The military bands of France were generally patterned after those in Germany; but in England, a new era was emerging with the increasing use and improvement of the clarinet. Although the clarinet was developed in Germany, it was the English bands that exploited its superiority over the oboe as their principal melody instrument. The clarinet became a leading military band instrument in England while the oboe, which had replaced the shawm in Lully's French bands, was relegated to second place. However, except for the addition of the clarinet, English bands still used the same basic instrumentation as those in Germany.

In 1783 the Duke of York imported a band of musicians from Germany to become the Band of the Coldstream Guards. This group eventually included two oboes, four clarinets, two horns, two bassoons, a trumpet, and a serpent. Several years later trombones and percussion were added, making this one of the earliest "modern" bands on record.

In 1789 a French conductor named Sarrette selected forty-five musicians from other bands and orchestras and formed the Band of the National Guard. A year later this band was enlarged to seventy players, and was supported by the city of Paris. Sarrette was succeeded as conductor by the leading French composer of that time, François-Joseph Gossec, while Charles S. Catel, another well-known composer, was his assistant. This group later disbanded and became the nucleus of the Conservatoire National de Musique (the Paris Conservatory) in 1792.

Instruments were undergoing constant and decisive changes and improvements: the flute had become conical, and therefore tunable; in 1832 Theobald Boehm perfected his ring-key system; the oboe had replaced the shawm; and in 1812 Blumel developed his piston valve, which, of course, revolutionized the world of brass instruments.

Through the efforts of composers and the work of the inventors, designers, and craftsmen of the late eighteenth and nineteenth centuries like Blumel, Stoelsel, Boehm, Klosé, Buffet, Wieprecht, Heckel, Sax, and others, wind instruments improved, becoming more consistent and reliable.

By the time Wilhelm Wieprecht (1802–1872) became leader of his Prussian military band early in the nineteenth century, the cornet and the trombone had already successfully joined the military band and the woodwind section had finally begun to resemble those of today. Wieprecht became very dissatisfied with the keyed bugles that were then in vogue and he abandoned these instruments in favor of brass instruments with piston valves. By experimenting with Blumel's piston valve, he was able to develop successfully the first satisfactory tuba. He was immensely successful and his band soon became the model for all Prussian military bands. His influence in developing a superior instrumentation was great and lasting.

Wieprecht may also be credited with planning and conducting one of the first Band Days comparable to our own fall American extravaganza. At a performance in 1838 honoring a visiting dignitary, he gathered together thirty-two bands totalling some twelve hundred musicians which he conducted with such success that the event was repeated four days later.

Adolphe Sax was a very successful instrument maker in Belgium and had already designed and built his successful bass clarinet before moving to Paris in 1841. In addition to inventing and building the saxophone which bears his name, he adapted an improved valve to all sizes of brass instruments which he matched out in a family called saxhorns. The instruments themselves did not represent new inventions; rather, they were an improvement and unification of the previously used alto horns, euphoniums, and tubas which had been difficult to blend or to play in tune. Our modern baritones and tubas have evolved from Sax's work.

Sax succeeded in persuading officials in the French government that his new revised instrumentation was superior to all others and the French government officially adopted his instrumentation for all of their bands. Since Sax owned all of the patents on the instruments and had the only factory which could supply them, his enterprise became a very successful monopoly. He became a wealthy man and his prominent place in the history of musical instruments was assured.

Bands in America

The Colonies to Patrick Gilmore

Throughout history we find that when there are great periods of significant artistic accomplishment, generally there are social situations which free the artist and patrons of art from the necessity of having to struggle daily for their existence. Such periods are characterized also by free communication and intermingling of different philosophies and schools of thought.

In the colonies of early America neither of these conditions was present. Instrumental music was a luxury not necessary for survival. Neither the Puritans nor the Quakers allowed bands of any kind. However, the Germans, Dutch, and Swedes did bring their old songs and their musical heritage to the new country with them. The earliest reference that we can find of a band performance in this country is in the 1630s when a Dutch band played in New Amsterdam, New York. Later, there are references to small German bands performing in Boston.

The first well-known band leader in America was a composer, performer, and concert manager from Boston named Josiah Flagg. In 1773 Mr. Flagg established a band of wind instrumental performers and gave several concerts in Boston, using a group of over fifty performers on one occasion.

It is interesting to note that before and during this time there were several British military bands in America. Their instrumentation included the clarinet while General Washington's forces usually had only fifes and drums—yet, these limited little bands were an important part of American military life, even in those times.

In 1775 the second Continental Congress met and General Washington was appointed Commander-in-Chief. While the Congress was in session Ethan Allen and his Green Mountain Boys were driving the British out of Fort Ticonderoga. After they captured the fort, history records that they celebrated their victory with a stirring fife and drum performance.

The American military leaders seemed to sense a need for some kind of music and since the Continental Army had neither band instruments nor musicians to play them, their martial music was of necessity provided by fifes and drums. Each company included a fifer and drummer, and their repertoire included such songs as: *The Rakes of Mallow, George Washington's March, The Georgia Grenadiers,* and others still found in fife and drum manuals.

Each regiment was allowed a "Fifer-Major" and a Drummer-Major" whose duties were to organize and train the musicians in the regiment. Later an Inspector and Superintendent of Music was added to the army and the level of performance improved quickly through scheduled practice sessions and better instruction. Rudimental drumming became an art which has continued to the present time.

George Washington was himself an amateur flutist and quickly recognized the value of fife and drum music for military purposes. In one of his papers he described a parade at Valley Forge in which the fifers and drummers played.

From 1796 through 1815 the Napoleonic Wars were raging in Europe. This caused many European musicians to come to the United States as refugees. During this period the Philharmonic Society in Boston was founded, and the foreign born musicians began to exert a strong influence on the musical life of this country through their teaching and performing.

In 1798 one of the great American bands was established. The United States Marine Band was born that year and was patterned after the European bands of that time. In 1800 it included two oboes, two clarinets, two horns, a bassoon, and a drum. Gradually its strength grew: in 1861 it included thirty musicians, and in 1899 it boasted of sixty.

There were a number of professional bands in the Boston area in the late 1700s and early 1800s. The Massachusetts Band of Boston was formed in 1783 and is thought to have become the Green Dragon Band, which later became the Boston Brigade Band attached to the Massachusetts Volunteer Militia. There is a record of another band called the Boston Brass Band which was particularly noted for its military appearance and fine marching. In 1842 the American Band of Providence, Rhode Island was organized with Joseph Green as leader.

Twenty-two years later David W. Reeves, the well-known march writer became the leader of the American Band in Providence. This was a completely civilian band, having no military affiliation or support. This band was basically a marching band, although it did give concerts, adding an oboe and a bassoon to its regular roster for those occasions. D. W. Reeves was intrigued by the musical possibilities of marching units and he is reputed to have developed what was called one of the greatest marching bands of all time.

Another man well known for his march writing, C. S. Grafulla, is credited with developing the first New York band having an instrumentation of reed and brass players proportioned so they could be adequately balanced. His band, the Seventh Regiment, N. Y. Militia, was organized in 1853, and in 1860 was renamed Grafulla's band. It is interesting to note that in the mid-1800s, the New York professional military bands were frequently engaged to play the commencement exercises of various colleges including Yale, Cornell, Harvard, Dartmouth, Williams, and Princeton.

Not to be outdone, the city of Philadelphia was also a center of band activity in the middle of the nineteenth century. Philadelphia had some of the best bands in the country from 1840 to 1860, and one of these units, known as Anderson's Band, enjoyed the reputation of being one of that city's finest marching bands.

Patrick Sarsfield Gilmore

The first American band leader whose influence in changing and improving the band allows him to be ranked with the great European leaders of the past was Patrick Sarsfield Gilmore, who has been called the Father of the American Band.

In 1854 Patrick Gilmore was a young and outstanding cornet soloist. (Up until this time most of the major soloists performed on a keyed bugle.) He was leading a band in Boston at this time and was invited to become leader of the Salem Brass Band, a position which he accepted in 1855. In a famous performance with this band, Ned Kendall, the acknowledged master of the keyed bugle, and Gilmore on his cornet played alternating strains of *Wood Up Quickstep*, a virtuoso show piece, in an effort to determine publicly the superiority of one instrument over the other.

In 1856 the Salem Brass Band became the first band from that city to march down Pennsylvania Avenue in Washington. The occasion was the inauguration of President Buchanan and a marching militia company, desiring the best available marching music, hired Gilmore's band for the parade.

He became leader of the Boston Brass Band in 1859, changing the name of the group to Gilmore's Band. With the advent of the Civil War he began leading parades and playing for recruiting rallies; much time was spent in these activities as the band marched and played in their colorful uniforms. In 1861 he enlisted his entire band with the Twenty-fourth Massachusetts Volunteer Regiment, accompanying them to the front.

Many of the professional bands enlisted with their local militia regiments. Some of the finest bands in the service during the Civil War included Gilmore's Twenty-fourth Massachusetts, P.V. Collis' Zoaves of Pennsylvania, Reeves' American Band, and Grafulla's Seventh Regiment Band from New York. Reeves' American Band headed the first group of the First Regiment from Rhode Island (which was the first Federal unit to be fully equipped and ready for duty) and is reported to have lost its bass drum during the wild retreat at Bull Run. All of the Union Regiments had bands, some of them containing up to fifty members.

Later, Gilmore organized and directed several immense festivals. The first took place in 1864 celebrating the inauguration of the Governor of Louisiana. For this occasion he mustered out a band of five hundred players!

His largest two festivals were presented in Boston where Gilmore was leading still another band. These events, in 1869 and 1872, were billed as Peace Festivals and they rank among the largest extravaganzas ever presented to the American public.

After the festival of 1872, Gilmore moved to New York, becoming leader of the 22nd Regiment Band. He began developing this group as a fine concert organization, established it as the finest band ever heard in the United States, and in 1878 led it in a European tour. He presented concerts in many of the great halls of Europe and although the band had an excellent reputation, its performance surpassed the expectation of even the most demanding critics. This band included sixty-two performers: two piccolos; two flutes; two oboes; one Ab piccolo clarinet; three Eb clarinets; eight first, four second, and four third clarinets; one alto and one bass clarinet; one soprano, one alto, one tenor, and one bass (or baritone) saxophone; two bassoons; one contrabassoon; one Eb soprano cornetto; two first and two second Bb cornets; two trumpets in Bb; two fluegelhorns; four French horns; two Bb alto horns; two Bb tenor horns; two euphoniums; three trombones; five bombardons (or basses); three drums and cymbals.

From time to time Gilmore enlarged the size of his band and by 1892, the year of his death, he was using a band of eighty-three players. While some of the instruments that he used are now obsolete, the instrumentation of his groups served as models for the finest bands that followed. Although he was influenced by the European bands of Wieprecht and Sax, he has doubtless earned the title of the father of the modern American band.

After Gilmore's death, Victor Herbert took over the leadership of the Gilmore Band and remained at that position for six years.

The well-known band leader Frederick Innes patterned his band very closely after the Gilmore Band in 1887. The band was called Innes' Great Band and it was quite successful. In 1889 an article in *Harper's Weekly* stated that there were over ten thousand bands in the United States, and in 1893 seventy-one bands marched in the inaugural parade for President Cleveland. It was obvious that the American band movement was well on its way.

John Philip Sousa

The natural successor to the Gilmore popularity and success was John Philip Sousa. Sousa was appointed conductor of the United States Marine Band in 1880 at the age of twenty-four and he enjoyed immense success with that organization. He resigned that position in 1892 (the year Gilmore died) to form his own band, and he seemed to continue the progress and success that Gilmore had fathered. Sousa continued to refine the band's sound, adding more flutes in place of Eb clarinets, and dropping the soprano saxophone, contra-bassoon, Eb soprano cornetto, fluegelhorns, and the tenor horns. He reduced the number of players in several of the remaining large sections; his first professional band numbered forty-nine players.

Sousa's reputation as a leader and composer of marches spread throughout the world. He toured Europe five times with great success and he made one tour around the world. It was in Europe that he was named "the March King." Sousa's band of 1924 had grown to seventy-five performers and it bore a remarkable resemblance to today's concert band. It included six piccolos; two oboes; one English horn; twenty-six Bb clarinets; one alto clarinet; two bass clarinets; two bassoons; four alto saxophones; two tenor saxophones; one baritone saxophone; one bass saxophone; six cornets; two trumpets; four French horns; four trombones; two euphoniums; six sousaphones; and three percussion.

18

Of course, Mr. Sousa is credited with the invention of the sousa-phone; however, his greatest contributions are the marvelous marches which he composed. His popularity was influential in creating a performance situation conducive to professional bands for several years. In those days—before radio, television, and other means of mass communication—bands were an important part of the American entertainment picture, playing at beaches, amusement parks, hotels, and resorts. Virtually any place attracting large crowds of people was a natural setting for a band performance.

Sousa   *Sousa and one of his early bands.*

As the popularity of the large amusement parks diminished and World War I arrived, we began to see the demise of the full-time professional band. As these bands began losing their financial support and started fading from the picture, instrumental music programs in the public schools began to make significant progress, and a new game appeared in the high schools and colleges called football. Also about this time (1923) a new concept of National School Band Contests and Festivals began to develop as the professional band almost disappeared.

It would be unjust and incorrect not to mention, however, that some of the finest of the professional bands did indeed survive. In New York, the Goldman Band continued (even to this day) to present its popular concerts in the city's parks. In Long Beach, the Municipal Band which was formerly led by Herbert L. Clarke still performs, and in countless cities throughout the nation civic and municipal bands regularly perform summer concert series.

Even more successful has been the continuation and growth of our finest military band organizations. All the major service bands in Washington, D.C. have flourished and probably provide today's finest opportunities for employment as professional band musicians. There are also many outstanding bands in other areas, specifically around the service academies and large military installations.

However, it must be agreed that, historically, the position of prominence in the public eye and the position of leadership in this profession passed from the military bands to the professional band during the life of Patrick Gilmore. So did it also pass from the professional bands to the school and college bands early in the twentieth century.

As the game of football became more and more an important sociological event in various colleges and high schools, the demand for better music and better entertainment at these events grew. The small, weak, disorganized bands during this embryonic stage began to develop and mature until they became well organized bands designed officially to represent their participating institution, continuing the old military band tradition, but, at the same time, adding many new outgrowths and refinements to the art of marching.

The thousands of high school and college marching performances presented each fall represent continuing efforts in precision marching, pageantry, and good solid music. All this is designed to entertain the public in the same basic sense that professional bands did at the turn of the century and military bands did before them.

Albert Austin Harding

Albert Austin Harding became director of bands at the University of Illinois in 1905. While his accomplishments reach far beyond the football field, he is credited with being the first leader to form letters and words on the field while playing. His University of Illinois band developed intricate formations for the performance of musical specialties such as had not been seen on the field before. He always insisted on *good* music, carefully prepared and accurately performed.

Mr. Harding is recognized as a pioneer in the movement which has made the appearance of bands an important part of the fall football spectacles. His university band set the standards, both musical and marching, for bands for nearly half a century.

Another important force just a few years later in 1912 was A. R. McAllister, whose outstanding bands at Joliet, Illinois earned a reputation for excellence that had never before been known in a school band.

Today there are outstanding college and high school bands in every area of the United States; the leaders of the last fifty years are too numerous to attempt to mention. Progress continues to be made: we are better organized, we have better music, we do more exciting drills, we use better equipment, we play in bigger and better stadiums. We have undoubtedly come a long, long way from our historic beginnings. However, we may actually have only begun to realize the artistic and entertainment potential of the modern band.

Summary

Colwell, in his book *The Teaching of Instrumental Music* states that "though the orchestra came into the public schools first, the marching band has been the vehicle through which the instrumental music program flourished, obtaining equipment, public attention, numbers, building space, and professionally trained teachers in a manner impossible for the concert band or the orchestra. Music has found a fairly secure place, not because it has caused a noticeable upgrading of musicianship in society or in the school, but because the marching band has publicized the school, attracted public attention, created excitement and spirit for competitive athletics, and made colorful holidays more colorful . . .

"The value of the marching band as a device for public relations and a source of enjoyment for students is a reality that the director cannot ignore, regardless of how much he prefers the concerts of the symphonic band or the wind ensemble. The marching band must have objectives and must be skillful—both in marching and in playing. The director cannot afford to feel that marching is an inferior part of the year's activities and one to be simply tolerated. Psychologically, the marching band is the students' first introduction to the year's activities. To wait for enthusiasm and interest to flourish with the first concert is hazardous—the group may by that time reflect a carelessness and negativenss produced by the chore of weekly football shows under a director who hates them."[1]

Frederick Fennell in his book, *Time and the Winds*, says that "The public appearances of school and college marching bands are the services by which the general public best knows and judges the value of institutional music. It is not surprising, therefore, that the first 'requirement' for the training of a college or high school band director in the eyes of the public and those who administrate its schools is his proficiency in the art of the marching band.

"In this regard, the public demands that the band should serve its truly indigenous function—that of playing out-of-doors on foot where other ensembles, which lack its mobility and acoustical projection, cannot function with similar success. This band provides, better than any ensemble of musical instruments, a workable medium of sound and cadence, supplies necessary color, and permits mobility for public events held in the open air. For these purposes it is as completely equipped as any musical ensemble in existence. It is for this express purpose that it was conceived and, in turn, developed by the military of early 19th century Europe.

"The outdoor band has a distinguished musical literature to which the composers of almost every Occidental culture have contributed generously and without persuasion. This band has the acoustical fabric required for the accomplishment of its purposes. This band has a relatively standardized instrumentation. This band has organization in the extreme, it has distinguished leadership, and it exists and functions with unbelievable success in almost every community in the United States. But this is the band which many high school supervisors and college band directors are anxious to pass on to an assistant or to eliminate entirely from their activities. The admirable purposes inherent in such possibilities, however, may never come to pass for it is unimaginable that there are many conductors who can deny themselves the genuine pride of conducting the "Alma Mater" on a crisp autumn day while from 10,000 to 200,000 eyes recognize them as the admired and respected conductor of the band which has just entertained them."[2]

1. Richard J. Colwell, THE TEACHING OF INSTRUMENTAL MUSIC. © 1969. Reprinted by permission of Prentice-Hall, Inc., Englewood Cliffs, New Jersey.
2. Used by permission of the G. Leblanc Corporation, Kenosha, Wisconsin, sole owner of the copyright.

2
Introduction to the
Basic Principles

The following portions of this book are designed to provide teachers with the practical knowledge, basic skills, and specific devices which will enable them (1) to teach a band to march, and then to march and play; and (2) to conceive, design, prepare, and teach a show or marching band performance.

Certain decisions have to be made before one can really begin, otherwise the teaching and rehearsing may be disorganized and without direction. Some of the decisions will be based on necessity due to various factors in a particular situation (number of band students, size and height of stadium, playing ability, etc.) and certain decisions are simply a matter of individual preference or taste (whether to march 8 steps to 5 yards, or 6 steps to 5 yards, [pp. 45, 46] ; whether to be a fast tempo, high knee lift type band; a slower tempo, more stately, military style band; a corps style band; or some combination of several styles.)

There must be a basic knowledge of the field on which you will perform and a basic organization of your band *outside*, just as there is *inside* with a concert band. This should provide you with an orderly base of operations. Once the organization is structured, it is necessary to know and be able to execute the fundamental moves which are utilized in most basic maneuvers or drills. For greatest efficiency, success, and progress, it is essential that the moves and their names be standardized for the band, allowing what is done throughout the marching season to be consistent and orderly. This results in realization of continuous progress in marching and playing skills and in mastery of the difficulty and sophistication of the maneuvers attempted.

When the teacher utilizes the basic concepts and fundamental moves explained in subsequent chapters and learns their abbreviations (your writing vocabulary, p. 59), he will then be prepared to teach correctly and successfully, as well as effectively perform the drills or maneuvers which are explained as Multiple Option Drill Techniques in chapters 6 through 11.

The various drills which are explained and illustrated are not intended to be an exhaustive, complete list of every possible type of maneuver. Rather, they are examples of some of the most successful types of drills, each utilizing different basic concepts and presenting a different visual appearance. The drills can be used precisely as explained and illustrated; or, they can be used as examples which may serve as a starting point from which the teacher can exercise his own creativity and ingenuity, creating his own drill to fit his own music and the band.

Basically the plan of this portion of the book is to provide:
A. Concepts and principles necessary to function properly on a football or band practice field.
B. Devices necessary to perform drills and maneuvers, and how to teach them.
C. Examples of drills and formations, and how to perform them.
D. Techniques to put these all together for a finished show.

Having a good band and being in a good band are very satisfying and great fun. Our sincere hope is that this book will provide information, ideas, and/or inspiration to those who seek or need it, and that in some way it may contribute to helping all of us provide our students with a better, more exciting and satisfying musical experience through the Marching Band.

Basic Principles

Attention to Details

One of the most important facets of any fine band performance is meticulous attention to details. Everything that each bandsman does on the field is vitally important. *There are no last chair players in a marching band.* On the football field, the visual arena is so large and complex that, while no one can see everything going on, any member of the band may at some point in a show be observed closely by someone in the audience, especially now that television closeups are so common. The attention of the audience is immediately drawn to a bandsman who is not completely uniform in every move he makes. Absolute uniformity without errors or goofs requires a 100 percent effort by 100 percent of the band, 100 percent of the time. Uniformity is a *must* in a fine marching band.

Uniformity, or precision (which is uniformity in motion), is a result of individual discipline, or self-discipline, and this kind of discipline is a result of desire and pride. Students have to *want* to march and play well . . . they have to be motivated! No teacher, or director, can produce an outstanding band unless the students in that band want it to be good. A marching band (especially a "drill" band), like the proverbial chain, is only as strong as its weakest link.

Everyone in our audiences can recognize a straight line. It is probably much better and wiser to perform simple maneuvers and drills superbly well while playing with a good sound than to attempt material which may be exciting in concept but which is too complicated and difficult for the group to do well.

Preparation

A great amount of planning and preparation normally goes into every good half-time production. Formations and drills should always be worked out prior to the first rehearsal. They should be checked and double checked on charting paper, and formations should be checked on a model football field with "little men" when possible. The drills should be charted and written down very carefully, including every move each bandsman is to make, then written out and duplicated as instructions for the band. This allows instruction on the field to take place in the most efficient manner possible. However, students must be encouraged to *read* and study the charts. With practice and experience groups can become very expert at following written drill and formation instructions, as well as working under their section leaders or rank leaders in marching rehearsals. (Further explanations and illustrations of charting are included in the units on Specific Drill Devices, Drill Techniques, and Formations.)

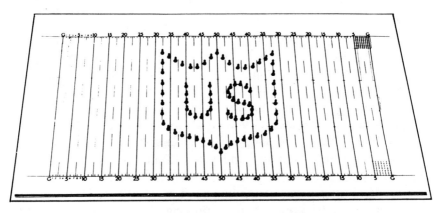

Example of a plotting board with magnetized "little men."

There are good bands that produce half-time performances in ten or more hours of regular rehearsal a week; but other groups can accomplish similar performances in much less rehearsal time, because the director has spent much more of *his* time in preparation before the first rehearsal. It *may* take ten hours for a band to learn one new drill. However, if the teacher would spend five hours in personal preparation, writing down on chart paper every move by everyone in the group, giving each of them every move he makes, it may be possible for the band to learn the drill in *five* hours. And if the teacher would spend seven hours preparing—making absolutely certain that everything "worked," that there were no errors either in the drill, the charting, or the instructions—it is conceivable the drill could be learned in *three* hours. The key lies in the preparation of the band director.

Much of the criticism we hear about marching band by administrators, parents, and students is directed at the great amount of student time lost during football season as a result of standing around on a practice field learning a new show. Much of the wasted time could be eliminated by more careful and more thorough planning by the teacher before the students ever get outside. Also, many of the bad performances that we witness, which result from groups not having quite learned the show, could be avoided by better teacher preparation *before* and *between* rehearsals. Such teacher preparation and discipline would result in much more efficient use of the students' time.

We frequently hear marching bands criticized. We are told that they take too much time, or that they are "not relevant." This criticism is misdirected! Marching bands are *not* necessarily irrelevant, and do *not* necessarily take too much time. It is not the marching band that is bad, but too frequently the marching band *teaching* that is bad!

Too many marching band teachers spend precious rehearsal time "working out" details and, indeed, whole drills and formations which should have been completely worked out and checked and rechecked before the band attempts them outside. The day has passed when we can enjoy the luxury of having students stand around a field while we decide what to do next. Today's students are the brightest, best informed group of young people in history and their most precious commodity is time. They have more to do and more to learn than any group of students in history; if we abuse and waste their time through inadequate teacher (or director) preparation and selection of bad or irrelevant music, perhaps we deserve to lose them.

A marching band can be a truly satisfying experience for the performers; but there must be a sense of accomplishment and there must be a feeling of success. Lost or wasted rehearsal time defeats both of these objectives and results in a loss of momentum that is very difficult to overcome. It is the responsibility of every teacher to spend enough time in preparing the band's show so that the performances are perfected in a minimum of rehearsal time, thus effecting the most efficient and productive use of everyone's "band" time.

3
Fundamental
Movements

Fine precision marching can be accomplished only through the mastery of fundamentals. These basic details of marching must be taught first to the individual. Each individual must have a complete understanding of all fundamentals that are used in his band, and, through concentrated drilling, must learn to execute each fundamental correctly. Absolute uniformity of carriage (how one holds his body, head, shoulders, instrument, etc.) and motion must be continually stressed, and every effort must be made to eliminate any individual differences.

The fundamentals which shall be described and suggested in this book are concerned with the basic moves and positions necessary to attain flexibility. This flexibility enables anyone to take advantage and succeed at most of the standard drill techniques and devices which have evolved for today's marching band; they make your band a *multiple option marching band*. These are not *limiting* techniques; they are *broadening*, or expanding techniques, allowing bandmasters to take advantage of innovative ideas as they evolve.

Block Band Positions

In the stationary basic block band each member is in one of three formal positions:

1. *At Ease*—Right foot remains in place; *no talking*. This is the command given to relax the band while it receives instructions. Also, this is the position that should be taken upon hearing the command "Fall In," or "Block Band."

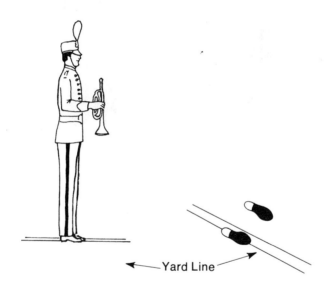

At Ease

2. *Attention*—Heels and toes together; body erect; place thumb knuckle of free hand against trouser seam; cup hand slightly (bending fingers from the middle joint); raise chin slightly. When standing at attention, the arch of the foot is on the line, centering the body over the line. Because of the varying lengths of players' feet, it is recommended that neither the toes nor heels are as practical for fine alignment as the suggested arch. There is no movement or talking in this position.

Fundamental Movements

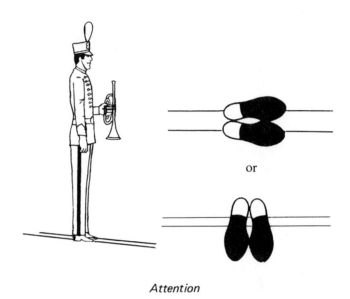

or

Attention

3. *Parade Rest*—is a position long used in many bands. If it is
   used, talking may be allowed in the position of *At Ease,* and
   there will be no talking at Parade Rest. *Parade Rest* is used to
   break the rigidity of the position of attention in order to give
   instructions or relax when a parade has stopped. Feet comfortably apart—with right foot remaining in place, and left
   foot moved out to the left. Free hand (if there is one) is
   placed behind the back—hand comfortably closed, with the
   back of the hand touching the small of the back. This author
   prefers not to use this during normal field rehearsals.

Front   Rear

Parade Rest

Instrument Carriage

Pre-game and *Half-time*—There are many varying ideas and styles of carrying instruments. Perhaps the safest and most uniform method is to hold all instruments with two hands at all times. This solves the problem of what to do with the otherwise free hand. The instrument will then be either: (1) straight up and down at a right angle to the ground, in the center of the body (from left to right, except saxes and sousaphones); or (2) in proper playing position.

In *parades* (such as those entering some stadiums)—all instruments are held in the left hand, as determined by rank leaders, leaving the right hand free to swing uniformly and normally.

31

Stationary Commands

It is imperative that all commands and responses be in strict cadence. The command should establish the tempo of the cadence, which should then continue consistently until the command or maneuver is executed.

The basic stationary commands have a verbal response. This can be very helpful: it is a good teaching device, it is good show business, and, it *does* attract the attention of the audience.

The following commands are necessary to most marching styles. Their execution and style vary according to the needs of various bands. However, there are definite advantages to using certain devices and rules, and these are included in the explanations which follow.

A. *Attention*
   Command: "Band"
   Response: "Band"
   Command: "Ten-hut"
   Response: (Shout in cadence) "One, Two."

On the count of "one" raise left knee sharply until the thigh is parallel to the ground. It is important to raise the leg by lifting the knee, leaving the toe anchored to the ground as long as possible as the knee is raised. Lift the foot from the back of the heel, "peeling" it off the ground. The foreleg is parallel to the right leg (which has not moved) and the toe is pointed toward the ground.

As the left knee is raised, arch the back slightly and lift the chin. On the count of "two," place the left foot sharply down beside the right foot, keeping the back arched slightly and the chin raised. The heels *and* toes should be together, body erect; place thumb knuckle of free hand against the trouser seam and cup hand slightly (bending fingers from the middle joint). This is now the position of attention.

It is therefore, a four count sequence:
Preparatory command: "Band!"
Response: "Band!"

1	2	3	4
"Ten-	Hut"	"One!	Two!"

"One!"
(Foot up)

"Two!"
(Down)

Attention

B. *Right Face; Left Face*

    Command: "Right Face," or "Left Face"
    Response: (Shout in cadence) "One, Two."

These are military facing movements which turn a group or an individual in the simplest way 90 degrees to one side or the other. On the count of "one," execute the indicated turn. On the count of "two," bring feet sharply together. Note: for Left Face, turn on left heel and right toe. For Right Face, turn on right heel and left toe.

1	2		3	4
"Right (or L) Face!"			"One! (Pivot)	Two!" (Close)

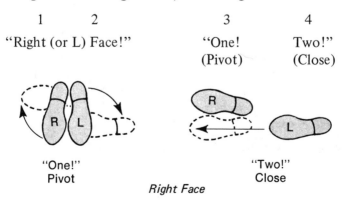

"One!"
Pivot

"Two!"
Close

Right Face

33

Fundamental Movements

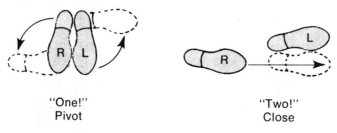

"One!"
Pivot

"Two!"
Close

Left Face

Half left; Half right face: same as above, but the turn is only 45 degrees.

C. *About Face*
   Command: "(A)Bout Face!"
   Response: (Shout in cadence) "One, Two."

This is also a traditional military facing movement. On the count of "one" place right toe behind and to the left of left heel. On the count of "two" pivot (turn around) on left heel and right toe, turning to the right. (When teaching this, it is sometimes helpful to have the student lift his left toe off the ground before pivoting.) If the right toe is properly placed, the turn will be completed with feet (heels and toes) together.

1	2	3	4
"(A)Bout	Face"	"One!	Two!"
Command		Response	

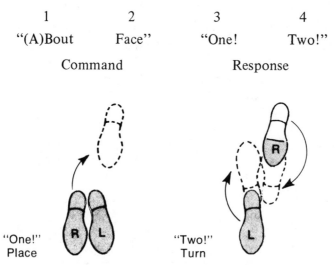

"One!"
Place

"Two!"
Turn

Traditional About Face

Cross-over About Face

This popular variation of the traditional About Face has enjoyed much use and success. It uses the same command and response as the military About Face previously discussed.

On the count of "one," place right foot to left side of left foot; on the count of "two," pivot on both toes, turning left.

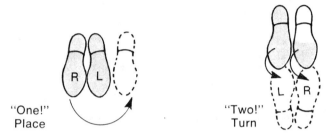

"One!"
Place

"Two!"
Turn

Cross-over About Face

Three Count About Face

A third variation, or type of About Face is popular with some excellent bands and corps. This move uses three counts, and consequently obviously uses three moves.

On the count of "one," take a normal 22½ inch step forward with the left foot, placing it in front of and slightly to the right of the right foot; on the count of "two," pivot on both toes (or on the ball of the feet), turning to the right; on the count of "three," the left foot moves smartly to a position of attention beside the right foot.

1	2	3	4	1	2	3
"(A)Bout"	(wait)	"Face"	(wait)	"One!	Two!	Three!"

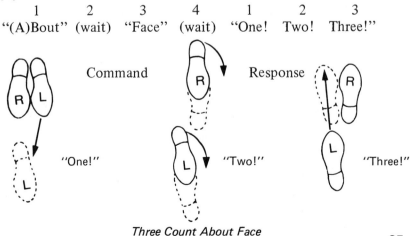

Command   Response

"One!"   "Two!"   "Three!"

Three Count About Face

D. *Raise Instruments*

It is necessary to establish a uniform way to move instruments to playing position. Some bands do this as quickly as possible after the command or whistle. Other groups do this as a two count, a four count, or even an eight count maneuver.

1. This command may be "automatic" after stopping in place in fanfare position for pre-game or half-time. Executing such movement after a "Halt Cadence" would be:

Hit and Close and   Up!

("Hit and Close" is the device used to "halt," or stop marching— see page 49.)

On the command, "Close" the free hand goes to the instrument.

On the command, "Up" the instrument is raised sharply into playing position.

Doing this *on* the "Halt Cadence" would be like this:

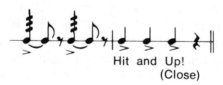

Hit and Up!
(Close)

NOTE: An interesting variation of the automatic raise instruments is to make the "raise" a slow deliberate uniform move of eight counts. This is especially effective as a sudden change of pace after a particularly fast and flashy entrance.

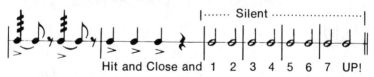

Hit and Close and 1   2   3   4   5   6   7   UP!

2. As a stationary command, Raise Instruments must be by counts and may be either a verbal or a whistle command. There is no verbal response. There is a four count preparatory command:

Counts:	1	2	3	4	1
Verbal:	"Raise	Instruments"	(wait)	(wait)	UP!
Whistle:	Long	Short	(wait)	(wait)	UP!

If the right hand is not already on the instrument, raise it to the instrument on the count of two. *Freeze* on the "waits" (counts 3 and 4) for maximum impact, and raise instrument as quickly and sharply as possible on the count of 1.

3. When marching and playing a parade the Raise Instruments must be automatic after a "Raise Instrument Roll-off" (which must be completely different from the "Halt Cadence").

The Roll-off may follow a drum cadence or street beat with no break, in which case the band raises instruments on the 5th count, or the first beat of the second set of 4 counts, with the free hand coming to the instrument on the 2nd count.

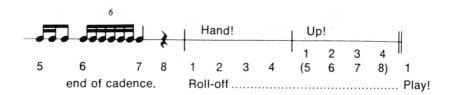

A more interesting and safer way to set up the Roll-off is to precede it with 4 counts of silence, with the instruments raising on the first count of the Roll-off, like this:

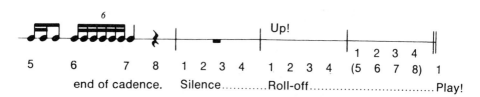

37

Fundamental Movements

After a strong drum cadence, four beats of silence is sometimes easier to notice than a different rhythm or pattern. Also, this gives the players eight counts to get ready to play, enabling them to begin playing with maximum strength.

Three Roll-offs:

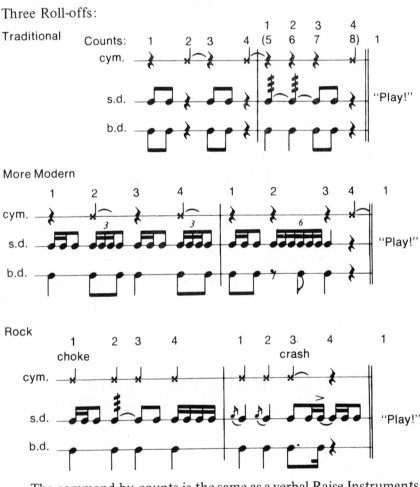

The command by counts is the same as a verbal Raise Instruments:

1	2	3	4	1	2	3	4
"Raise	Instruments"	(wait)	(wait)	UP!			

Again, if there is a free hand it goes to the instrument on the count of 2.

E. *Instruments Down*

Just as it is necessary to establish the procedure for *raising* instruments, it is also important to establish how and when instruments should be *lowered* from playing position. We call this command "Horns Down," and when we use it, we add it immediately after the release of the last note of a piece of music, such as:

play-off, "Horns Down"   or   hold-off, "Horns Down"

Lift instrument slightly on "Horns." Bring instrument down sharply on "Down."

F. *Vocal Response*

When the performance situation is unusually noisy, as at the beginning of a half-time show, the preparatory command, "Band," is given by the drum major, or director, to assure the band's attention before an important command. (It is always given before "Attention" at half-time.) When this command is shouted, it is to be echoed by the entire band. Lower the voice in the throat, and shout all verbal responses.

The importance of standardizing all fundamental movements cannot be over-emphasized—either in oral presentation or in written instructions. Many bands have serious precision and execution problems simply because they are not being asked to execute a specific maneuver or movement with consistency. A *To the Rear, Left Face, Right Face,* or *Forward March* should be the same at the end of the marching season as it was in the beginning, unless it is being deliberately changed in order to achieve some special effect or improvement.

Mastery of these fundamentals by every member of the band is a major step toward achieving that uniformity and precision which are the goals of many bands and teachers. It also provides the group with the necessary moves that are required to accomplish most types of marching drills and routines. The chapters that follow present myriad drills and marching devices which have proven to be both very effective and easy to prepare.

4
Building a
Half-time Show

Half-time shows come in many styles, types, and sizes. In order to provide a starting point for the new teacher who is not sure how or where to begin, we shall start with a very basic format which can be easily followed and developed into good entertaining marching band performances. Such performances can be both musically satisfying and educationally valid.

A show must have a *beginning, development, feature number(s), climax* and *exit*. One way this can be accomplished is through the following basic sequence of action:

Entrance (to fanfare formation, normally using drum cadence)

Fanfare

Downfield March (to get to the center of the "stage [field] area")

Precision Drill Routine (using appropriate thematic music, drilling into a concert formation)

Musical Feature (played from concert formation; may feature one section soli, or may also serve as a number for a feature twirler, or drill or flag squad of some sort; perhaps, feature them to the side the band is not facing)

Formation (saluting someone, something, or some music; again this can be a good place to present majorettes, flags, etc. If they were featured facing one way in concert number, place them on the other side for this number. Later in the season as the band learns more and longer drill routines, this section [formation] might be omitted to allow a longer Precision Drill Routine section.)

School Salute (forming the name or initials of the school; and
exiting with the school's most popular fight song)

There are many ways in which this basic format can be expanded,
extended, made more complex, or varied for the sake of interest.
By carefully selecting your music and ideas (drills and formations),
a well executed performance in this basic format can be very pleasing
and satisfactory to both audience and performers.

The number of ways a band can enter a field, or present a fanfare
or drill is, for all practical purposes, infinite. The variety of appearances is limited only by the imagination and ingenuity of the person
designing or developing the show.

Develop a Style

Many outstanding marching bands have developed an audience of
fans that follow the progress and success of their favorite band with
the kind of enthusiasm and loyalty enjoyed by top-flight athletic
teams. Most of these bands have a readily recognizable style with
which their audience identifies and looks forward to. Schools with
British or Scottish mascots or themes have natural, built-in styles.
But there are many cases where the reputations and following of
bands grew as their styles of performance developed and became
more clearly defined. Many geographic locations and/or school
names suggest styles or themes with which fans can readily identify.

Pick a style that appeals to you and that is appropriate for your
school and band; then work to develop it. Refer to it in your press
releases and scripts; use it in your P.A. (public address) announcements. You might find (or write) a fanfare and/or downfield march
that identifies, or ties in with your style.

Field Organization

The Football Field (for high school and college stadiums)

Since half-time performances take place on a playing field which
is especially designed for a specific athletic contest, and which is
generally regulated by various conferences or leagues, there are
certain features of this field that remain constant and can be used as
guide points in planning and executing marching performances.

The goal lines are 100 yards apart. This 100 yards is divided by yard lines at intervals of five yards, and these five yard intervals can be readily divided into eight 22½ inch steps (called "8 to 5"), or six 30 inch steps (called "6 to 5").

Goal posts are placed 10 yards behind the goal line, and the area between the goal line and the goal posts (or the goal post line) is called the end zone. There is no marking at the minus five yard line in the end zone. The goal posts are 23 feet, 4 inches wide, measured from the inside.

The playing field is 160 feet wide. Inserts, or "hash marks" are placed 53 1/3 feet in from each sideline, dividing the field into three equal parts. Both the hash marks and the yard lines may be used as guides, and both are invaluable. (See illustration on page 43.)

The Basic Block Band

Outside rehearsals are best begun from the position of the *block band*. This provides every bandsman with a permanent marching assignment and identity. It simplifies the checking of attendance by utilizing one student (rank leader) in each rank to report on the absence in his rank; it simplifies and expedites getting the rehearsal started by providing a pre-determined starting point, or a "fall in" position.

By assigning permanent identification numbers and letters to the positions in the block, communication, both verbal and written, is greatly simplified, thus making the preparation and use of written instructions, drill charts, and formations much more practical.

The basic block band consists of *ranks* and *files*. Ranks are those lines of bandsmen which run from right to left. Ranks are lettered, A, B, C, etc., starting with the front row of players and continuing to the back of the band. Files are those lines of players which run from the front to the rear. Files are numbered 1, 2, 3, etc. Thus, everyone in the block can be identified with a letter (rank) and a number (file); such designation indicates the person's position in the block. The right and left sides are determined from the *player's* point of view. For example: The person on the right end of the first row (rank) will be the first person in the first file (from the right). He is in "A Rank" and he is also in "File #1." His designation, or permanent identification number, is "A1." A person in the second

Field Diagram

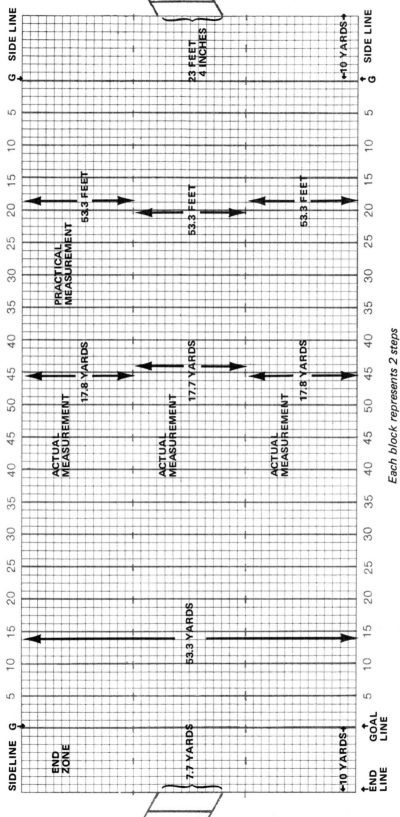

Each block represents 2 steps

43

line from the front, and the third person from the right is designated
"B3"; the person in the sixth line from the front, and the fifth
person from the right will be "F5." In this manner all regular members of the marching band have a permanently assigned position in
the block. The players can then go to their basic block band positions for warm-up and music rehearsal while attendance is being
checked.

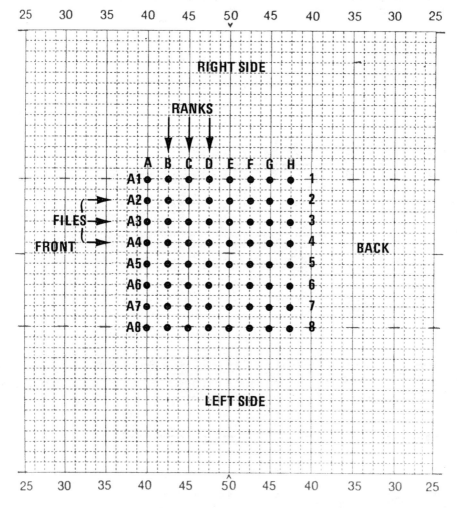

Block Band, 8 Ranks by 8 Files
Total: 64 players

Each person standing in the block is 2½ yards from the next person in any direction. Odd numbered ranks (A, C, E, G) are on five yard lines, even numbered ranks (B, D, F, H) are one-half way between the yard lines.

With eight people across (an 8 man front), place the outside bandsmen on the "hash marks" (or one-third insert markers), and evenly space the six people in between these outside points.

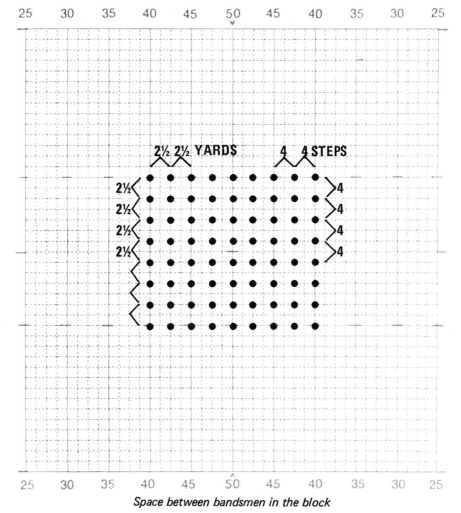

Space between bandsmen in the block

● *equals bandsmen.*

4 steps equals 2½ yards.

Each little block represents 2 steps; 8 steps per 5 yards.

Alternates may be added as an extra rank in the rear of the band; in this way they may take part in playing and in fundamental drill practice. They may be designated the next letter after the last rank (I), or X rank, or whatever is appropriate.

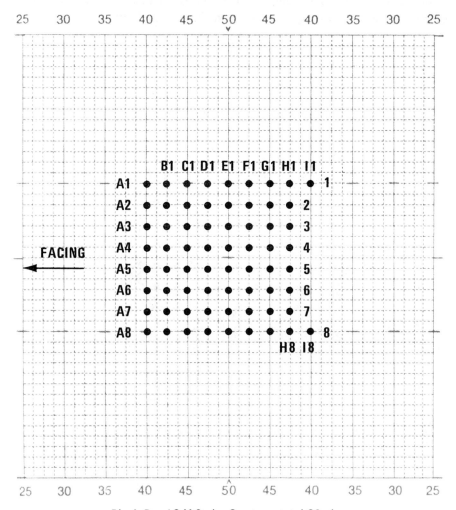

Block Band 8 X 8 plus 2 extra = total 66 players

The basic block may be either a square or a rectangle with the length exceeding the width. For best proportions and appearance the length should not be more than one and one half times the width.

A block consisting of 8 ranks of 8 players is a beautifully symmetrical unit of 64 players. This 8 player front is an ideal block for bands of under 100 members. Between 100 and 150 players, a ten player front (or ten files) may be used. Perhaps the most desirable unit (after a block of 64) is a block of 12 x 12. The 12 player front (with two players placed outside the hash marks on each side) is ideal for groups of up to 196 performers.

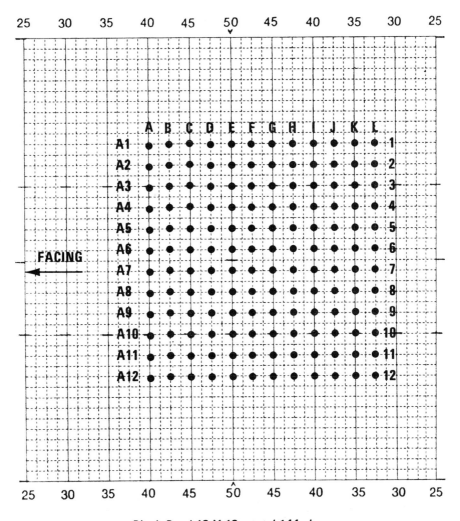

Block Band 12 X 12 = total 144 players

Rank Leaders

Every rank should .have a rank leader. It is wise and practical to select an older, more mature musician-marcher in each rank to perform this important function. This person works in the "chain of command" below the elected band officers (if such have been designated) in rank. Both the officers and the rank leaders work under the drum major, who, of course, is responsible to the director. These student leaders can serve as genuine teaching assistants. With the use of a fundamental check list, each one can (with proper preparation) be responsible for the marching skills, appearance, and performance of the students who are in his rank.

Rank leaders can:
1. Check the attendance of their rank which they, in turn, give to the band secretary.
2. Teach and drill fundamentals, thus enabling better individual attention through work in smaller groups.
3. Help establish the route of their rank into a formation. (The position in the formation is established by the drill chart.)

Use of Rank leaders:
1. Provides opportunities for students to develop leadership.
2. Encourages development of higher morale through pride in and identity with one's rank.
3. Allows instruction to take place on a much more personal level, by working in smaller groups.

The United States Marine Band in Block Band Formation

5
Moving
Down the Field

There are several basic decisions that every marching band director must make for himself. Perhaps the most fundamental of these is whether to march 8 steps to five yards, marching on the balls of the feet, lifting the knees, and pointing the toes; or, 8 steps to five yards corps-style, with no knee lift; or, to march 6 steps to five yards, using a "stride step." While it is possible, and even desirable, to mix the three styles (and many fine bands do this very well) it is advisable for new bands or new band directors to pick one style to start with, and to develop and refine it.

Frequently, new teachers make the mistake of trying to do too much, too fast, with the result being a confused band which does many things, but none of them well. Pick a style, and master it!

The second basic decision, especially if the choice is to march 8 steps to five yards, is whether to hit the (5) yard line with the left or right foot. There are many arguments for doing it each way and there are fine bands which are exponents of each system. Let's examine these.

Basically an 8 to 5 band which strikes the yard line with the right foot will make most of its turns on the right foot, usually on the counts of 4 or 8. Most of the turns and maneuvers will be executed either on a yard line, or half way between them. Using this system, drills can very easily be designed to fit the musical phrases (usually multiples of 8). The player makes the first step (left) in motion off the line, and a turn usually results in the first step in a new direction occurring on the first count of the new phrase. This results in greater impact on the audience.

Left footed bands step down on the yard line on the count of one, and step off the line on the second count with the right foot. They then strike every yard line with the left foot, usually on the counts of 1 or 5. The strongest argument for this system is that most turns now occur on the first beat of each measure, so the turns occur on strong beats. Two weaknesses of this system are that: (1) after an introduction, the band takes a first step, but it does not go anywhere until the next beat; and (2) the turns lack impact since the musical phrase begins while a turn is being executed and the new direction occurs on the 2nd beat of a phrase. This is psychologically weak.

The drills and instructions that follow are all based on 8 to 5 marching, with the right foot striking the line. Everything can be converted to left footed marching (with the left foot striking the line) very simply, and the drill principles are usable with any band, whether it used 6 or 8 steps between yard lines.

To Move Down the Field

A. Take 8 steps to every 5 yards (22½ inch steps).
B. Strike the yard line with the right foot, stepping off the line with the left. As you cross a line the *ball* of the foot strikes the line.
C. When taking 8 steps to every 5 yards and striking the yard line with the right foot on the count of 8 (or 4 if one starts halfway between the lines), it takes more than 8 counts to move the band five yards. On the 8th count the right foot does strike the line; however, the left foot is still not in place. To facilitate halting the band, we automatically add the words "Hit and Close" on counts 9, 10, and 11, as explained under Moving Commands (see page 52). So, the command and counts necessary to move the band five yards are:

4 whistles (in tempo)   , 8 counts, Hit & Close.
Beep, Beep, Beep, UP (push off with right foot), Go, 2, 3, 4, -8, H & C.

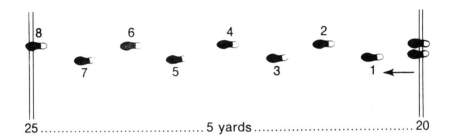

D. *All* changes of direction are executed on the *right* foot.
E. When marching down the field—maintaining a straight direction of march and maintaining accurate spacing from left to right—use peripheral vision while keeping the head erect, the eyes focused straight ahead, and approach and cross the yard lines at a perfect right angle. In other words, march down a field route that is perpendicular to the yard line.

To Move Across the Field

A. Size of step remains constant (since the exact measurements going across the field are slightly larger, the step should be slightly larger than 22½ inches, and is called an adjusted 22½ inch step).
B. Guide to the files which you cross at a right angle, if part of the block remains.
C. Guide to the 1/3 inserts, or "hash marks," whenever possible. From the sideline to the nearest hash mark is 28 steps, and from one insert to the other is 28 steps.
D. When marching down a yard line, center your body over the center of the line. Make the center of the chalk line an imaginary line between your left and right foot.

Moving Down the Field

8 steps/5 yards

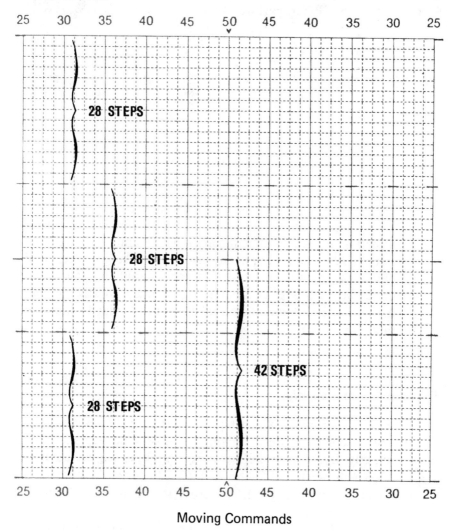

Moving Commands

A. Forward March

This command is given only from the position of Attention. The command is four short whistles in cadence. These whistles establish the tempo of marching and music. On the fourth whistle, the left knee is lifted in a preparatory knee lift. The position of the left knee on the fourth whistle is like the count of "one" of Attention. Raise the knee so that the thigh is parallel to the ground, the foreleg is parallel to the right leg, and the toe is pointed towards the ground; "push off" with the right foot, raising slightly on the right toe. On the first beat after the 4th whistle, the left foot strikes the ground 22½ inches in front of the right foot.

"Beep," "Beep," "Beep,"   "Up!"   "One,"   etc. ....

Forward March

Automatic Forward March

If you wish to play an introduction in place and start forward motion on the first beat of a first strain, or the first beat after the intro, this must obviously be established with the band—preferably the very first time that the drill music is rehearsed. All bandsmen should mark their music in pencil indicating "stand" at the beginning of the intro, and the initials for Forward March, FM, at the appropriate place. In this way much of the risk will be taken out of the maneuver and valuable rehearsal time saved. In this case, the band would have to be at attention with instruments in playing position, the 4 whistles simply would indicate the tempo; playing commences on the first beat after the 4th whistle. Hence the preparatory knee lift occurs on the last beat of the introduction, or, the beat immediately preceding the first forward step.

53

Moving Down the Field

Broadway Salute

George M. Cohan

Arr. by Robert E. Foster

4 whistles (Beep, Beep, Beep, Beep):

Play (Stand fast, don't move).............................Up, ┌─┐Go! 2, 3, 4,

STAND   FM

B. Hit and Close

This is our basic halt command. It is a three beat addition to a strain of music or to an even number of steps and facilitates a halt at a given place with the right foot. (Note: to move a bandsman five yards or 8 steps, it is necessary to add something, since on the count of 8 the right foot has arrived at the stopping point, but the left foot is not yet there.) On the first additional count, "Hit": the left foot strikes (or hits) in place beside the right foot as the right foot is lifting off the ground. On the second count, "And": the right foot strikes in place as the left foot swings out and slightly foward from the hip. The left knee and ankle are straight! On the third count, "Close": the left foot is snapped down sharply beside the right foot. Note: Upon first entering the football field just before the fanfare, on the command "Close," the free hand (if there is one) goes to the instrument. This securely positions the instrument for a sharp "Raise Instruments" which will follow, and both hands will remain on the instrument until the conclusion of the show.

Two additional "halts" are used with great effectiveness. Some bands use these or a variation of these for their basic "halt," however, the author prefers using the Hit and Close for the basic or standard "halt," while using other halts with increasing frequency for special effects (see page 55).

1. Stomp Halt—this is a simple halt in which the left foot is placed sharply in place beside the right foot on the next count after the right foot arrives at the halt position. For example: If the right foot is in place on the count of 8, the left foot "stomps" in place beside the right foot on the count of 1 which follows.

"8"   "Hit"   "And"   "Close"

Hit and Close

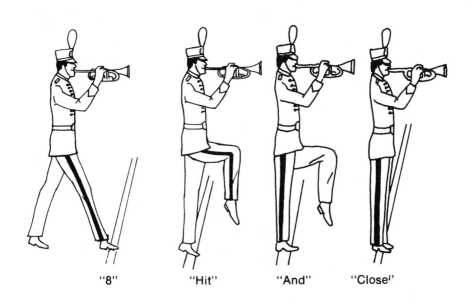

"8"   "Hit"   "And"   "Close"

A Second Optional Hit and Close

2. Corps-style Halt—this is a one count halt like the Stomp Halt, except that the left foot is placed down approximately 22½ inches parallel and to the left of the right foot.

This places the band in a good solid "feet apart stance" which is particularly effective for playing out big endings and finales. For an even stronger ending, have all instruments raise (toward the press box) at a 45 degree angle—either instantly at a given point in the music, or gradually in a big crescendo towards the finale.

Counts: 5, 6, 7, 8, 1

Verbal: L R L R Stop!

C. Mark Time

Begins just like "Forward March" (with the fourth count a preparatory knee lift), then march in place, lifting the knee and pointing the toe downward. Be careful to step down with the toes first on each step. By keeping the raised toe pointed, the foot can be kept more flexible—much less stiff than landing flat footed—and can serve as a "shock absorber," making it possible to play well while the feet and legs are in motion.

Some bands mark time by just lifting the heels off the ground while leaving the toe anchored to the ground. This is a fast way to achieve uniformity, and is smoother and less likely to be bouncy enough to hurt the playing. Many persons, however, prefer a mark time which is more active and vigorous like the one first described.

D. Left Flank

This is the device used to change the direction of march 90 degrees (a right angle) to the left. Execute this by turning on the ball of the right foot and raising the left leg similar to the move on the preparatory 4th whistle of Forward March. On the next count the left foot strikes the ground in a full 22½ inch step in the new direction (see page 57).

E. Right Flank

The device used to change the direction of march 90 degress to the right, again turning on the ball of the right foot. This is commonly executed two ways:

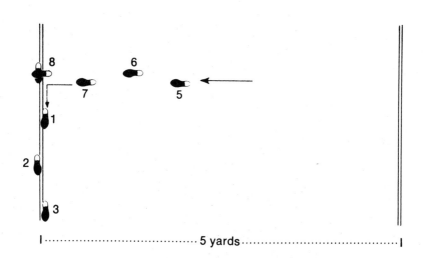

Left Flank—Individual Routing

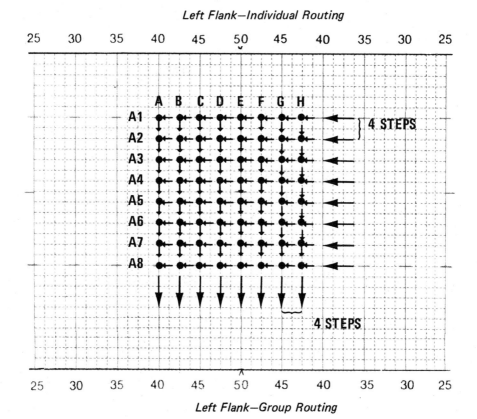

Left Flank—Group Routing

57

Moving Down the Field

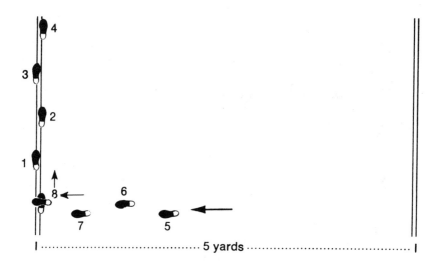

Right Flank—Individual Routing

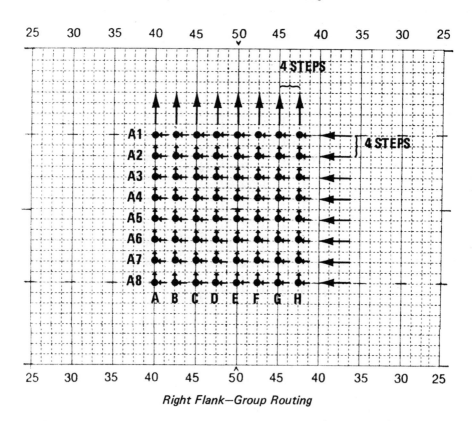

Right Flank—Group Routing

1. Cross-over—the traditional, more military move in which the left foot must "cross over," with the left knee raised as described above, stepping in the new direction on the next beat. (See illustrations on page 58.)
2. Spin Turn (¾ Turn)—This is a more flashy maneuver and eliminates the awkward cross-over just mentioned. It is used *only* on right flank movements. The right foot strikes the yard line; the player then spins vigorously around counterclockwise in a ¾ circle, the next step being a full 22½ inch step to the right with the left foot.

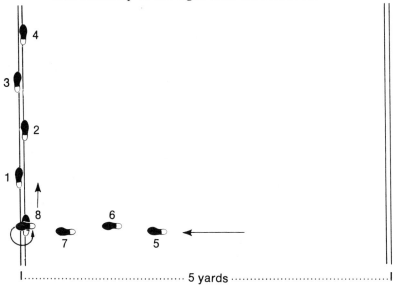

Right Flank—Spin Turn—Individual Routing

F. To the Rear

This provides a change of direction of 180 degrees. Place the right foot directly in front of the left foot (using a normal length step), and pivot on the balls of both feet counterclockwise (with heels lifted), keeping back (left) foot anchored to the ground. When direction is reversed the left foot is already in place for the next step, eliminating the problem of getting a uniform "first" step in the new direction. Note: Left, or Right Flank, and To the Rear are usually executed on the right foot on an even numbered step, producing a change of direction on the next count. By using a device known as a *Delayed Pivot*, the maneuver may be executed on the very end of the even count after a sudden "freeze"—with the pivot occurring suddenly and instantaneously almost on the beginning of the next count.

Developing these turns requires much effort and attention to detail. This kind of turn is quite difficult on the Flank movements that would ordinarily involve a cross-over. They are most practical and most easily taught when maneuvering "To the Rear," since both feet stay anchored on that turn and the next step is already set by the left foot. To teach To the Rear, or to rehearse it pivoting on the right foot after the count of 8, say: "1, 2, 3, 4, 5, 6, 7, STOP (freeze), TURN! 2, 3, 4," etc.

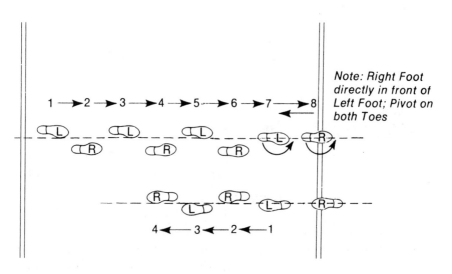

To the Rear

Specific Drill Devices or Maneuvers

A. RIGHT or LEFT BY SQUADS
   This is an eight count move using SQUADS of four players, standing side by side at a two step (45 inch) interval. Normally, the pivot man is the #1 or the #4 man. The pivot man

will usually mark time in place, gradually turning (in place) as the rest of the squad swings around him to the left or right in a "pinwheel" type turn, using 8 steps for every 90 degrees, or ¼ circle, turned. The standard two step spacing must be maintained throughout the turn.

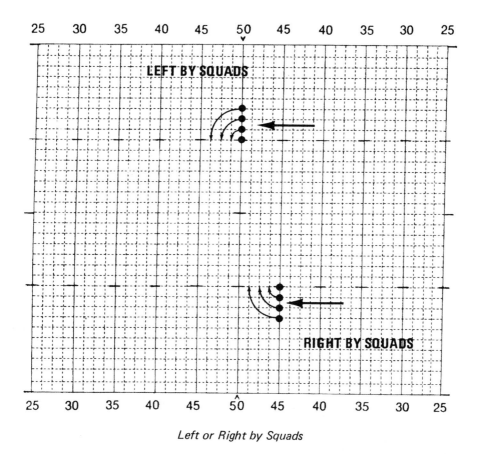

Left or Right by Squads

The pivot will ordinarily be (1) STATIONARY—with the pivot man marking time and turning in place. However, it may also be (2) MOVING—with the pivot man moving 45 inches (or two steps) to the right or to the left during the wheeling movement. This serves to move the entire squad two steps in the desired direction, so that each man in the squad has moved over one "space." The third type of squad

61

move is with the (3) CENTERED pivot—with the pivot man executing his pivot so that he arrives at a position one step (22½ inches) from the imaginary pivot point on the yard line. This moves the entire squad one step, or 22½ inches, to its right or left as it swings around. It also enables up to four squads to revolve evenly around the same pivot point, as required in some popular four-man squad drill concepts.

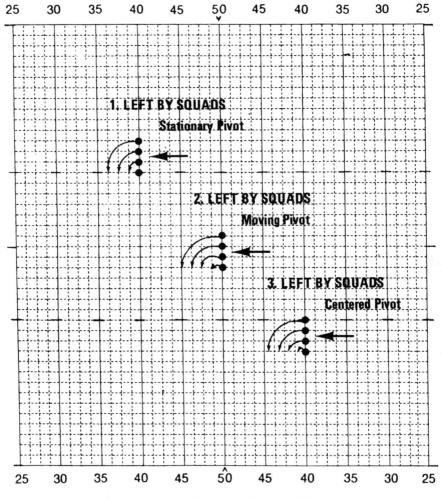

Stationary, Moving and Centered Pivots

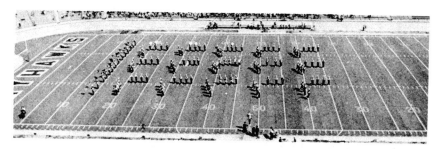

Drill illustrating Left by Squads—Stationary Pivot

B. Progressive Movement (Step Ones, Step Twos, or Step Fours) forward, to the rear, or to either flank:

Each player in a line steps off at an interval of 1, 2, or 4 counts, doing a specified maneuver. An example would be "Forward March 8; To the Rear 8 by Step Twos." The first marcher in a line would step off in a Forward March; two counts later the next person would step off, and every two steps a new person would step off until all have stepped off the line. Each would march forward 8 counts, execute a To the Rear, and return to the line from which he began. Step Ones alternate the foot of execution (every other person is on the left foot, or the right). Step Twos and Step Fours all "push off" with the right foot, the first forward step (22½ inches long) of the maneuver being with the left foot. This device (progressive movements) is most effective when done from company fronts (long single lines) with bandsmen waiting to step off. A bandsman may mark time or stand fast, whichever the teacher specifies, while waiting for the other persons to finish (see page 64).

Moving Down the Field

Drill Example

Progressive Movements

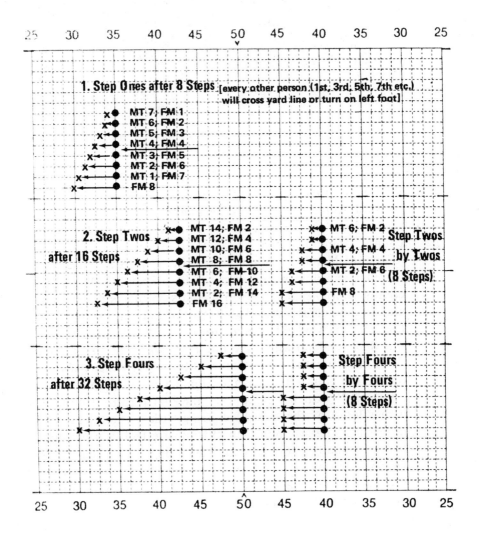

● = STARTING POINT
x = STOPPING POINT AFTER 8 COUNTS
MT = MARK TIME
FM = FORWARD MARCH

64

C. Rank Leader Drill

This is a device for getting to a specified position in a formation. The Rank is under the leadership of the Rank Leader, who may be asked to determine the route and the drill maneuvers used in route to a new position. The routes to a new position may be specified or they may be freely structured, thus allowing the Rank Leader to devise and teach an original drill sequence or move (see page 217).

All moving commands and drill devices may be used by Rank Leaders in establishing routes, or they may be specified on drill charts. Each bandsman is expected to know these maneuvers by both name and abbreviation.

Abbreviations

The abbreviations themselves are necessary for two purposes:
1. To shorten and simplify writing instructions on drill charts.
2. To use in marking music either at the music rehearsal, or before the first outside rehearsal.

FM	Forward March
MT	Mark Time
LF; RF	Left Flank; Right Flank
TR	To the Rear
L/S; R/S	Left by Squads; Right by Squads
SP; MP; CP	Stationary Pivot; Moving Pivot; Centered Pivot
8-16, etc.	The number of steps, or counts, in a maneuver
RL	Rank Leader (as in RL Drill)
H & C	Hit and Close

Drill charts, therefore, may look something like this:

A Rank: FM 16; R/S 8; MT 8; TR, L/S 8; FM 16; TR, MT 8; H & C

Translation:

The first rank (A Rank) marches forward 16 counts; executes a Right by Squads 8 counts; Marks Time 8 counts; turns To the Rear, and executes a Left by Squads for 8 counts; marches forward 16 steps, turns To the Rear again, Marks Time 8 counts, and Hit and Close in exactly the same position from which they began.

Moving Down the Field

Note: While this means of communicating may seem complicated and difficult at first, students and teachers throughout the country have discovered that it is a very efficient and practical way through which to communicate. Any group can adapt to this system quickly, and it does provide a common, consistent, and orderly means of writing down and communicating instructions.

6
Corps-Style
Techniques

The Corps Influence

The increasing visibility and impact of the competition corps has become a major factor in the continuing development of the marching band. This influence, and our reaction to it, has varied greatly from one part of the country to another, and from one institution to another. It has ranged from persons who "ignore it and hope it will go away" to persons who see it as "the new hope," and adopt it as completely as possible.

Probably most of us will fall somewhere between these two extremes.

The growth and popularity of corps cannot be denied, and their influence has resulted in some major changes in the appearance and impact of marching band performances.

Among the more obvious changes or developments are:

1. More public visibility and interest for marching shows as a result of the popularity of the Drum Corps International (DCI) televised competition. The success of this area is a direct result of the drive and organization of the DCI, which has set up standardized procedures, judging standards, vocabulary, and generally led the way in the re-emergence of the competition corps as a viable and important force on the musical scene.

67

2. Better pacing and change of pace. Again, the DCI has influenced the nature of the shows being presented, and as a result of this we are seeing more complete shows, planned as one entity rather than the sum of several unrelated parts. There is better flow and continuity.

3. More variety and less rigidity, both musically and in marching, as a result of a more sophisticated approach and more sophisticated techniques, including more use of arcs and additional playing positions.

4. More emphasis on staging, particularly in nontraditional forms (or formations).

5. More emphasis on rudimental drumming and the expanded percussion section, with new standards of performance and uniformity, as well as increased emphasis on using the percussion section creatively (see the DCI manual of regulations and interpretations).

6. Increased emphasis on better use of more auxilliary units: flags, rifles, color guard, etc.

7. More emphasis on special arrangements and arrangements with more built-in contrast of dynamics, texture, and tempo and style. There is new emphasis on musical considerations, again, with the DCI rules and standards being a major force for this.

Corps-Style Fundamentals

The ultimate goal in corps-style marching, as it should be in other styles of marching, is absolute uniformity in all moves and maneuvers. While most of the more commonly used corps-style fundamentals are consistent with those which have already been discussed, there are certain other facets of these fundamentals which are common to most corps, and which are utilized in many corps-style bands.

A. *Attention*

While bands may do this exactly as the examples earlier in this book, it is required that corps in DCI competition use the traditional military attention with the heels together and the toes separated (from 30 to 60 degrees).

B. *Parade Rest*

This is the same as in the earlier description (page 30).

C. *Playing Position*

While the basic playing position is the same as those shown earlier, there are two additional playing positions which are used with great effectiveness.

1. Horns Up (or Horns to the Box)—this is essentially the same move discussed in the earlier discussion of the Corps-style Halt. The instruments are raised so that they are 45 degrees above the normal level position, which results in dramatically improved projection. This is most effective when used to emphasize emotional peaks or climaxes. Proper use of this move adds drama and visual impact to your performance. (Students will need to be shown how to do this. As they raise their instruments, they will need to throw their head back and arch their back.)

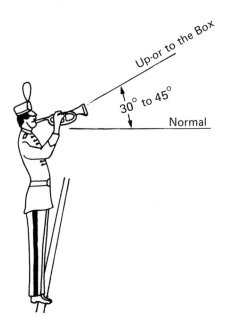

Horns Up or Horns to the Box

2. Horns Right, Horns Left, or Horns Center Stage—this device is also both a visual and a musical move, enabling the players to project their sound toward the stands while marching laterally or at an angle to the sidelines. These moves are most effective when used judiciously to enhance what is happening musically. Their impact is lessened by constant (or over-) use.

Horns Right

D. *Facing Movements*

Most corps and corps-style bands use traditional facing movements as discussed in Chapter 3.

E. *Halt*

This varies somewhat from corps to corps, however most corps or corps-style bands use some variation of the Halts discussed in Chapter 5.

F. *Mark Time*

The traditional corps or corps-style band uses a distinctive Mark Time that is usually referred to as "heel to knee" or "heel to calf." In both of these, as in the Mark Time dis-

cussed earlier, it is important to keep the toe pointed toward
the ground so that the toe, or the area immediately behind
the toe (the ball) strikes the ground first, with the foot then
"rolling" from the ball to the heel.

Mark Time—Heel to Knee   *Mark Time—Heel to Calf*

G. *Stride Step*

One of the most distinctive features of a fine corps-style band
is the smoothness with which they march. This effect is
achieved through mastery of the corps-style stride step.

This style of marching is particularly effective when using
a 22½ inch step, marching eight steps to five yards, however
there are successful bands and corps which use this style with
various lengths of stride, ranging from less than 22½ inches
to 30 inches (six steps to five yards).

The stride step uses no knee lift. The traditional "8 to 5
knee lift" is inappropriate for this style of march. Beginning
with the first step, every effort is made to keep the foot
parallel to the ground, and every step is made to a "flat heel"
with the foot rolling from heel to ball—in direct contrast to
the Mark Time where it rolls from ball to heel.

Do not "pick up the foot or knee." Instead, the foot is extended in front to a point 22½ inches forward and in line with the center of the body, with the center of the heel (not the back as in traditional 6 to 5 marching) striking the ground first, and the foot rolling to the ball of the foot.

A unique feature of this step is that each foot is placed directly in front of the other, similar to the effect created when someone walks a straight line.

The body is to remain virtually motionless from the waist up, eliminating all body movement in the upper half of the body. It is also bent back slightly at the waist, thus contributing to the appearance of dignity and smoothness. The smoothness of the stride step is conducive for better playing since there is likely to be less "bounce" and other unnecessary movement. (Note: When done correctly, there should be no "bounce" or up and down motion in any of the marching steps or styles—unless this is done for some special effect at some point in a show. An 8 to 5·high knee lift step done correctly should still leave the upper half of the body virtually motionless).

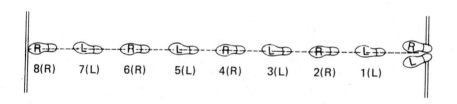

22½ Inch (8 steps to 5 yards) Stride Step

H. *Left Flank; Right Flank; To the Rear*
   These moves are essentially like those discussed earlier.

I. *Specific Drill Devices*
   Any or all of the drills in this book, or variations of them, may be used by corps-style bands, however, the use of squads (usually four persons) is much more important in corps and corps-style bands than it might be in other bands.

In corps-style bands, the squads sometimes function more as single units. They utilize the squad moves described in this text, but they also use a number of other devices very effectively. Among the additional devices which they utilize are:

1. Square Turns   2. Oblique Turns   3. Minstrel Turns

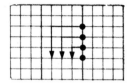 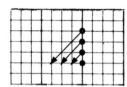 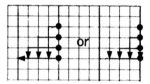

A corps-style Centered Pivot differs from the one used earlier. It is as follows:

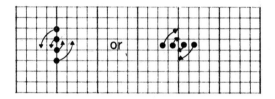

In addition to utilizing many of the drill concepts discussed in this book, corps have literally led the way into new, exciting, and effective drill concepts. The circle drills which are now used everywhere are a direct outgrowth of this "corps" influence.

J. *Curvilinear Forms*

These are designs formed by curved lines. A circle is a curvilinear form. Other curvilinear forms include arcs, radials, and swirls. The most basic and most common curvilinear form other than the circle is the arc. Arcs offer another opportunity to vary the look of your band, and they are relatively simple to form. Unlike some of the more complicated circle drills, arcs may actually be more effective with a smaller band than with one which is too large.

An arc may be formed from a straight line in four steps as shown in Example 1 below. In this example the person on the 50 yard line will march straight forward using a full stride step, with the length of the other marchers' strides diminishing more as they are farther from the 50 yard line.

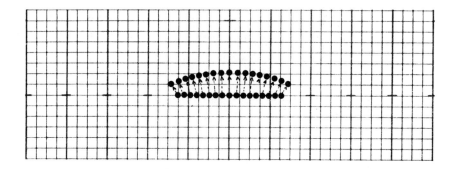

Example 1. Four Step Arc from a Straight Line

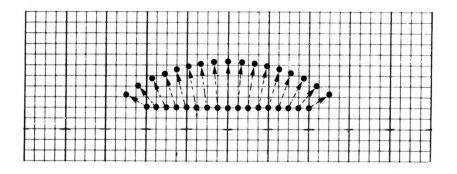

Example 2. Eight Step Arc from a Straight Line

74

Arcs may also be formed by the Follow-the-Leader technique as suggested for forming curved lines on page 217. Upon arriving in the arc position, it is important that every individual in the arc dress his interval very carefully, turning to face the proper direction at a pre-arranged time in the music.

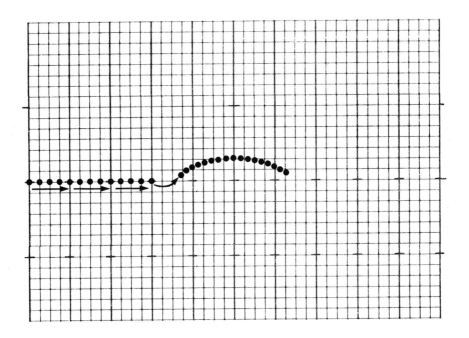

Example 3. Forming an Arc by "Following-the-Leader"

Just as the expansion of a circle is probably the most obvious and natural move to make after the completion of the circle, a similar move from the Arc, called the "Burst" is one of the most effective moves from the Arc. This effect is created by having all of the members of the Arc Forward March outward a given number of steps—their route being the same as that of the radii of the imaginary circle that the Arc would be a part of. The expansion of the curve creates a "bursting" effect.

75

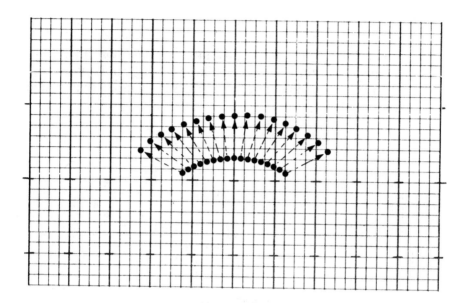

Example 4. A Simple Burst from an Arc

Musical Considerations

Corps through their competition shows have literally led the way to more interesting marching band performances. This has been accomplished because of several factors:

1. Very careful music selection.
   a. Using music with greater dynamic contrasts—higher highs and lower lows; music with stronger climaxes and endings, and which in itself generates excitement.
   b. More use of solo voices (and effective staging of them), thereby providing greater contrast in the texture as well as the volume and quantity of sound.
   c. More obvious use of more counterpoint and contrapuntal writing—contrasting with simple lines and simple textures.

2. Stronger emphasis on better coordination of the music and the drill, or of the drill to the music. Corps have clearly demonstrated the effectiveness of designing drills specifically for a given piece of music or arrangement, striving to create greater musical as well as greater visual effects than can be

76

otherwise achieved. The drill must fit the music and the mood of the music. Softer passages may very effectively be directed away from the audience, while the climaxes and strong sections are most effectively presented directly to the audience. These are the times when the direction of the instruments is of maximum importance.

3. Addition of special marching instruments for greater variety of tonal resources, particularly in the percussion section. The corps-style percussion section has grown to include the following:

Voice	Instrument	Description
Soprano	Snare Drum	This is your primary or "lead" percussion voice, and ideally there should be at least three of these.
	Tenor Drums	These are omitted from the corps-style percussion section; their voice, or role, being taken over by the tri-toms or timp-toms.
Tenor	Timp-toms	Different groups use up to three sets. Player(s) should have two sets of mallets, using soft mallets for certain soft sections or selections, and hard mallets for more projection and clarity—like on solo, or soli sections.
Baritone	Timpani	Marching timpani, tuned by handcranks, are being used with more regularity and more effectiveness. They are used in the same manner as concert timpani, and they should be played (correctly) the same way.
Bass	Bass Drums	More percussion sections are using three sizes (and pitches) of bass drums, rather than the traditional one size, or one large size and several scotch bass drums. These can provide additional variety in sound, but they also will require additional attention from the teacher to be fully and effectively utilized, providing a tonal bass line by playing separate but coordinated parts.

(continued)

Instrument	Description
Cymbals	The marching cymbal section has also been expanded, usually to either two sizes of cymbals—small (18 to 20 inches) and large (20 to 22 inches) providing two pitches, or to three sizes of cymbals—small, medium, and large, providing three pitches. As with the three sizes of bass drums, simply buying more equipment and playing it the old way will not improve or particularly change the sound of the percussion section. Many teachers will have to completely re-think their concepts of percussion sounds and work to create opportunities and musical situations which can fully utilize these new resources.
Mallet Instruments	Both xylophones and bells have been used with great effectiveness in corps-style percussion sections. They are played horizontally, and not upright in the old traditional manner. This enables the player to perform with much more accuracy and facility, using two hands to play as he would a concert instrument.

The Flag Line

One of the most striking facets of a fine corps-style band is an outstanding flag corps or flag line. When used properly these add a dimension to a marching performance that is very valuable.

Flags, or silks, provide visual motion. They can provide contrasting motion very easily and effectively: 1) flags go up when horns go down; 2) flags turn left when the band turns right; 3) flags can march through the band in contrary motion (flags go south when band goes north). Flags can enhance the drill, or dress up the drill, by joining the band—in front of the band, behind the band, or around the band; and flags can enhance the music by making moves which are appropriate and logical for the music and phrases being performed. Flags can be featured as a special unit, adding to the entertaining resources available to the director.

When preparing flag routines certain basic concepts and principles need to be kept in mind:

1. The flag routine (and movements) should reflect the tempo and mood of the music being played. Strongly rhythmic selections should be accompanied by strong rhythmic flag moves, while softer, slow ballads should utilize appropriately slower, smooth moves.

2. The sequence(s) of flag maneuvers should complement the phrase(s) of the music. Flags can reflect volume changes: for example going from soft to loud, by remaining almost motionless, and becoming increasingly busy, with bolder moves as the volume increases. During big finales, busy, bigger, and faster flag moves are called for.

3. Flags can effectively reflect other musical changes such as key changes, tempo changes, and style changes. Big flag moves accompany big changes.

It is the director's responsibility to provide effective settings for the flag line through thoughtful and careful staging. The flags cannot be featured well if they cannot be seen. It is just as important to provide opportunities in a show to feature the flag line as it is to feature the other units.

In stadiums where the audience is on both sides, or on both sides and in the end zones—as in a bowl, the flags and other auxilliary units provide a very important resource for providing more visual interest—particularly to those spectators who are not seated directly in front of the band on the press box side.

Vocabulary

Just as the organization of the Drum Corps International has standardized rules and regulations pertaining to DCI competitions, they have also led the way in establishing a standardized vocabulary, and as more and more bands adapt corps techniques and concepts, more and more band directors are using the corps' terminology when referring to marching bands.

Among the standard terms in use today are the following:

tick—a mark placed on a score sheet by a judge to indicate an error.

interval—the space between the centers of two marchers looking at them laterally.

space—the distance between the centers in the direction of depth.

cover—the straightness of a line of marchers from front to back.

dress—the straightness of a line of marchers looking at them laterally.

color guard—refers to the national color guard and all the silks, rifles, sabres, etc.

silks—flags.

pike—staff or shaft to which a flag, pennant or banner is attached.

weapons—sabres, side arms, lances, rifles, etc.

oblique—a movement or facing which is not perpendicular to the original line of march.

curvilinear forms—designs formed by curved lines.

military bearing, or *bearing*—posture properly carried out in a military manner.

sagging—the uneven compressing of intervals in an element making a turn.

fanning—the uneven expansion of intervals in an element making a turn.

band front—all nonplaying band members (flags, twirlers, rifles).

band proper—playing band member.

continuity—logical and orderly sequence of maneuvers and the compatibility of all marching details to each other to ensure a smooth entertaining presentation.

staging—proper placement of elements with respect to position and time to enhance the overall design of the show.

phasing ("out of phase")—an individual being slightly in front of or behind his line.

7
Multiple Option
Block Band Drills
Drill Techniques I

Since we began with the basic organizational structure of the Block Band, it is logical and appropriate that we begin our drills from that position. While simple in concept and easy to prepare and teach, these drills can be very effective, and the variations and developments of this basic theme can provide many interesting patterns and movements, all beginning from a starting position with bandsmen 2½ yards or 90 inches apart.

Block Band Drills

One of the most effective basic forms of drills which can be particularly appropriate for use with a young band, or a band early in the season, is Block Band Drills.

There are a number of advantages to starting with Block Band Drills:

1. This kind of drill is more conducive to a better sound, since players are grouped together, rather than isolated individually.

2. There is security in numbers! All moves are made by groups, and there is more safety in having larger groups of players

making the same moves than in having individuals moving separately.

3. It is easy to take advantage of the field markings, thus giving the marchers more help in maintaining proper spacing and alignment. This is not always available in drills utilizing more individual moves.

4. Most Block Band Drills can be performed beautifully using a minimum of fundamentals. To do these drills properly a band must know only four basic maneuvers:
   a. Forward March
   b. Left Flank; Right Flank
   c. To the Rear
   d. Hit and Close (Halt)

5. They can be charted easily, and taught quickly.

6. Adaptability: 1) These drills can be adapted to fit any solid music with normal musical phrases; 2) a block is very flexible —it is only four steps from company fronts (by moving the even numbered ranks forward four steps to the right of the person in front of them).

7. Effect: A continuing series of changing geometric patterns can evolve smoothly in kaleidoscopic effect. These can be successful even in stadiums with low bleachers.

These drills are simply a continuing division of the block into smaller units. These can then themselves divide into other units, the divisions joining together in various ways to form different geometric patterns. This works equally well changing divisions every eight or every sixteen counts. With a very large band, it is sometimes helpful to change every sixteen counts in order to get more distance between the different patterns.

The following is a very basic Block Band Drill for a 64 piece band using 32 counts:

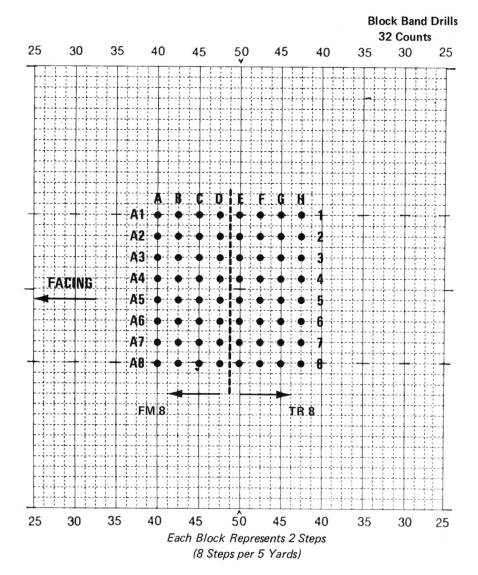

Each Block Represents 2 Steps
(8 Steps per 5 Yards)

Example No. 1—The band is facing in the direction of the long arrow (left). (The dotted line indicates the point at which the group will be divided.)

1. Ranks A through D: FM 8

   Ranks E through H: TR 8. Spin around on ball of right foot on 4th whistle of the four (preparatory) "Beeps." For example: Beep, Beep, Beep, Spin, Go, 2, 3, 4, 5, 6, 7, 8. Note: All turns preceding, or starting a move are executed in this manner.

83

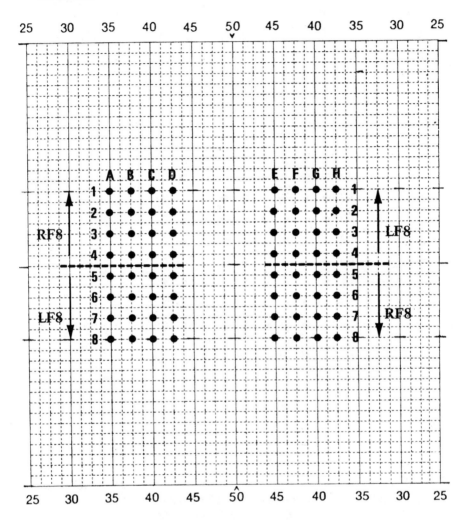

Example No. 2

2. A 1-4, B 1-4, C 1-4, D 1-4: RF 8 (Again, when teaching drill one step at a time, execute Flank Movement on 4th preparatory "Beep." Also, for added "Flash" use Spin Turns for all Right Flanks.

E 5-8, F 5-8, G 5-8, H 5-8: RF 8.

A 5-8, B 5-8, C 5-8, D 5-8: LF 8. Teach like the above, turning on 4th "Beep."

E 1-4, F 1-4, G 1-4, H 1-4: LF 8.

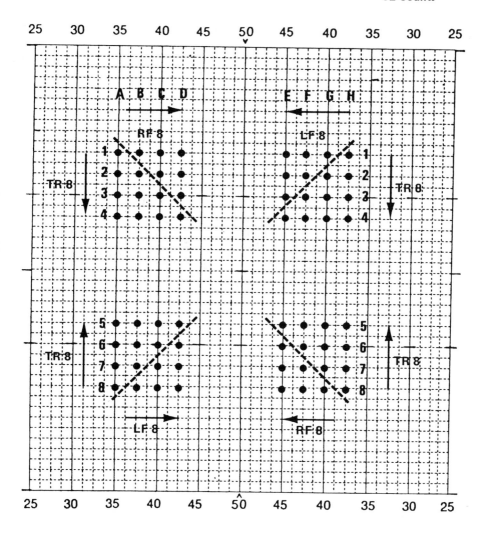

Example No. 3

3. A 1-8, B 2-7, C 3-6, D 4-5: TR 8.
   E 4-5, F 3-6, G 2-7, H 1-8: TR 8.
   B 1, C 1-2, D 1-3: RF 8.
   E 6-8, F 7-8, G 8: RF 8 (Spin Turn for "Flash").
   B 8, C 7-8, D 6-8, and
   E 1-3, F 1-2, and G 1: LF 8.

85

Block Band Drills
  32 Counts

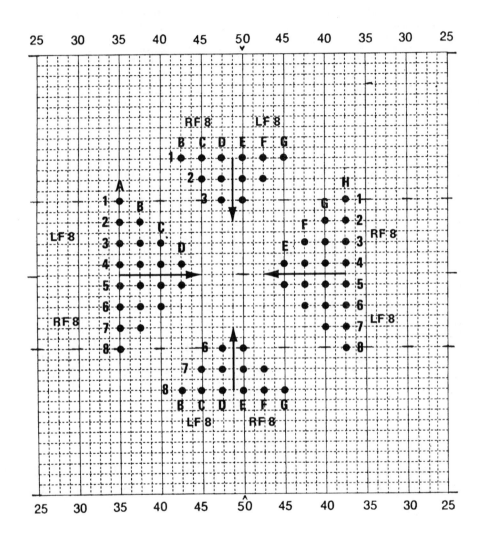

Example No. 4
    4. A 1-4, B 2-4, C 3-4, D 4: LF 8.
       E 1-3, F 1-2, G1:   LF 8.
       B 8, C 7-8, D 6-8:   LF 8.
       E 5, F 5-6, G 5-7, H 5-8: LF 8.
       All others: RF 8 (Spin Turn).

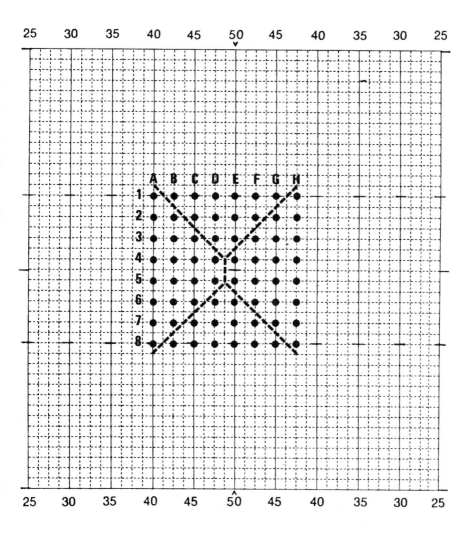

Example No. 5

(All have returned to block, and are facing the center—toward each other.)

The mimeographed Drill Chart for the above sample drill will look like the following:

Block Band Drill

Music: *Broadway Salute (Give My Regard to Broadway)* (or any song with 32 count phrases).

1. *Introduction* (In Place)
   All: MT 16

2. *Letter A*
   All A-D: FM 8.
   All E-H: TR 8.

3. All A-D 1-4's: RF 8 (Spin Turn).
   All E-H 5-8's: RF 8 (Spin Turn).
   All A-D 5-8's: LF 8.
   All E-H 1-4's: LF 8.

4. *Letter B*
   A 1-8, B 2-7, C 3-6, D 4-5: TR 8.
   E 4-5, F 3-6, G 2-7, H 1-8: TR 8.
   B 1, C 1-2, D 1-3: RF 8 (Spin Turn).
   E 6-8, F 7-8, G 8: RF 8 (Spin Turn).
   B 8, C 7-8, G 8: LF 8.
   E 1-3, F 1-2, G 1: LF 8.

5. A 1-4, B 2-4, C 3-4, D 4: LF 8.
   E 1-3, F 1-2, G 1: LF 8.
   B 8, C 7-8, D 6-8: LF 8.
   E 5, F 5-6, G 5-7, H 5-8: LF 8.

   All others: RF 8 (Spin Turn).

   (Diagrams like the examples may be used with the instructions.)

The same drill can be very easily extended to use 48 counts, as demonstrated in examples 1A through 7A.

Block Band—64 Players (8 x 8)   *No. 1A* . . . .

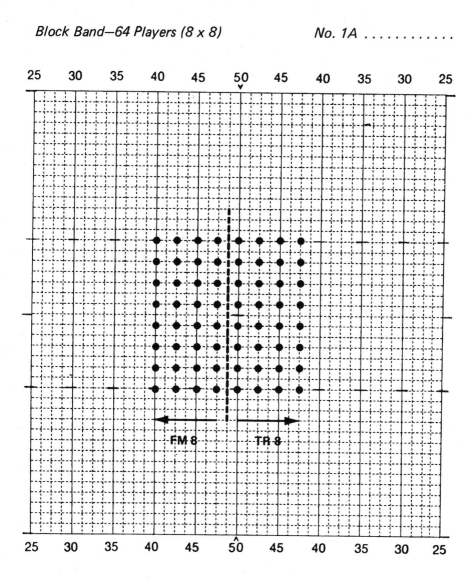

Block Band Drills
 48 Counts

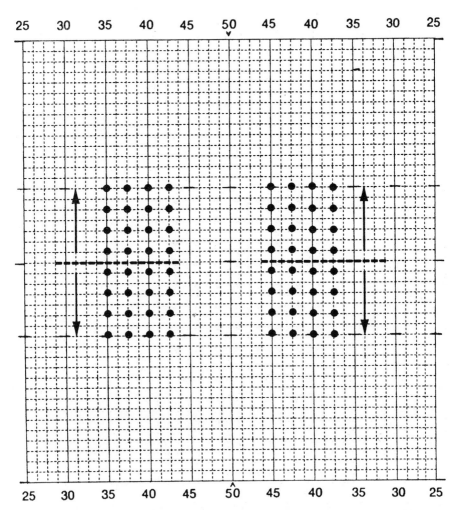

3A . . . .

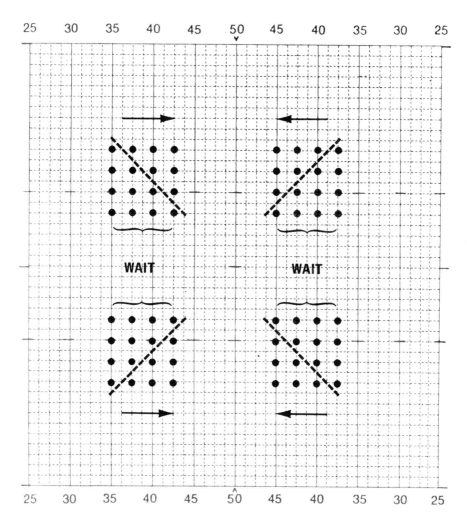

Block Band Drills
48 Counts

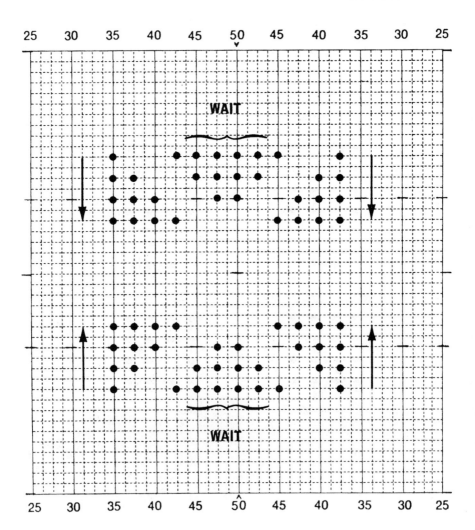

5A . . . .

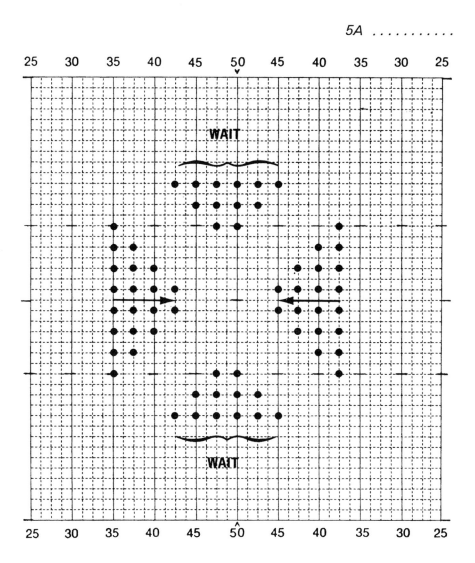

Block Band Drills
48 Counts

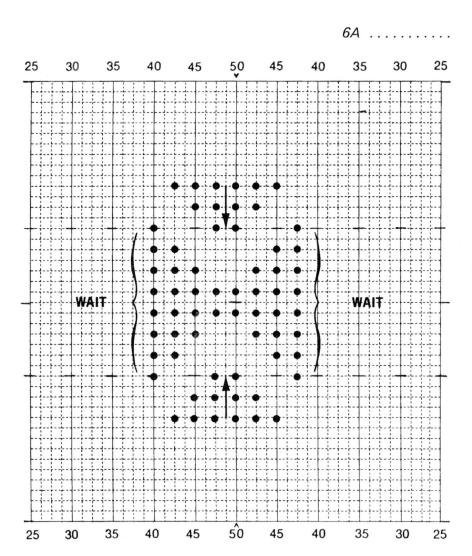

6A . . . .

WAIT

WAIT

7A . . . .

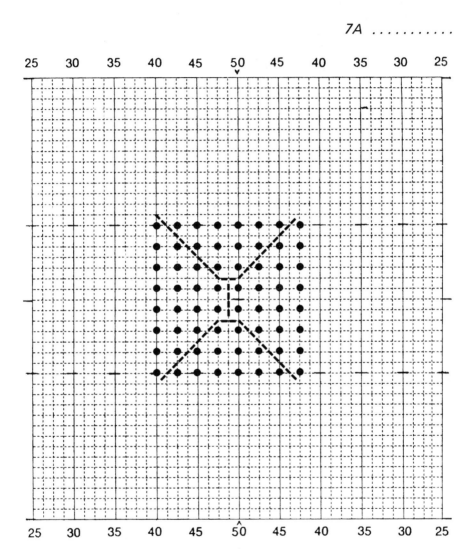

The drill can be varied so that the first move results in an "explosion" with each quarter of the band going in a different direction using the same number of steps or counts. This is shown in examples 1B through 3B.

Block Band—64 Players (8 x 8) No. 1B
Same Drill—Different Beginning

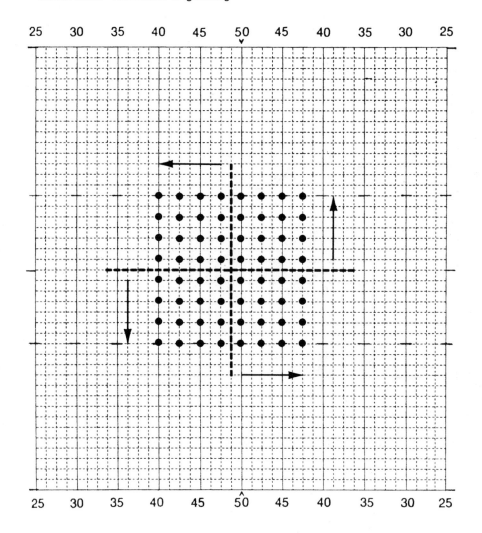

2B . . . .

25 30 35 40 45 50 45 40 35 30 25

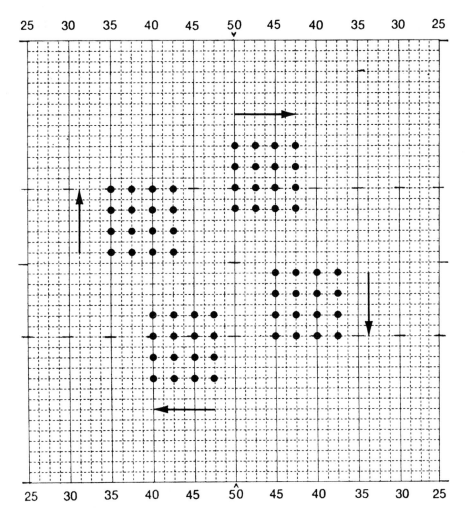

25 30 35 40 45 50 45 40 35 30 25

3B . . . .

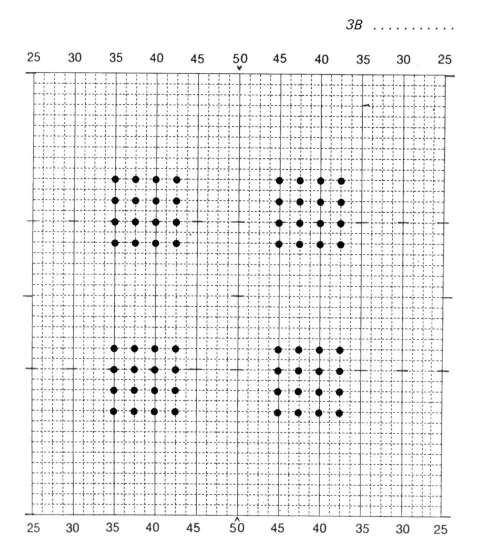

The remainder of this drill may be completed like 3, 4, 5; or 3A, 4A, 5A, 6A, 7A.

The best known block "explosion" (each quarter going in a different direction at the same time) is shown below. It is commonly called a "Block Buster."

Block Band Drill No. 1C

Block Buster Drill—64 Players (8 x 8)

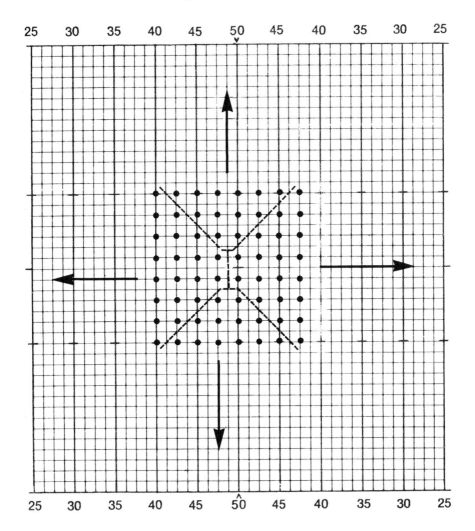

Block Band Drills

This drill concept can be adapted to any size band with very satisfactory results. Examples 1D through 4D illustrate some of the logical divisions that can be used with various sized marching units.

Block Band Drill No. 1D

Logical Divisions—48 Players (6 x 8)

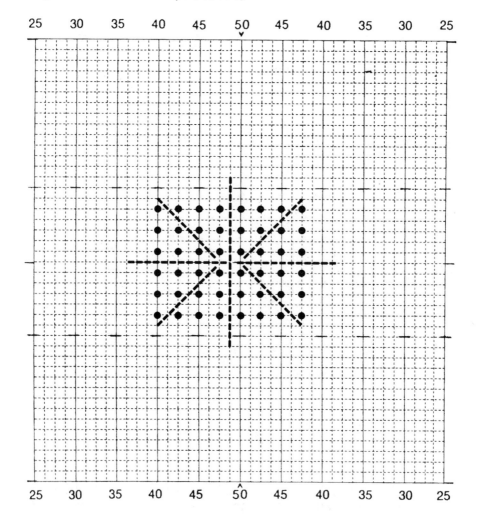

Logical Divisions—64 Players (8 x 8)

2D . . . .

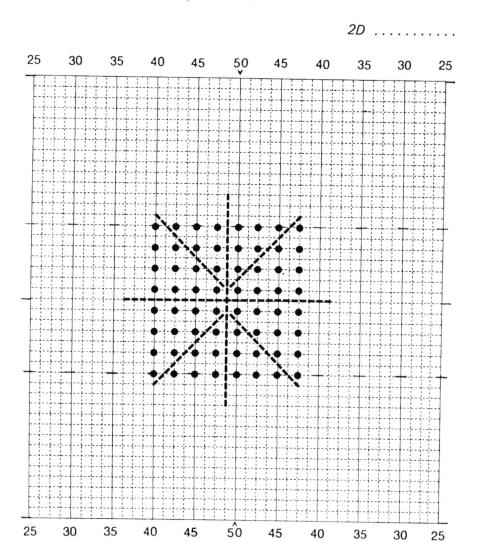

101

Logical Divisions—72 Players (8 x 9)

3D . . . .

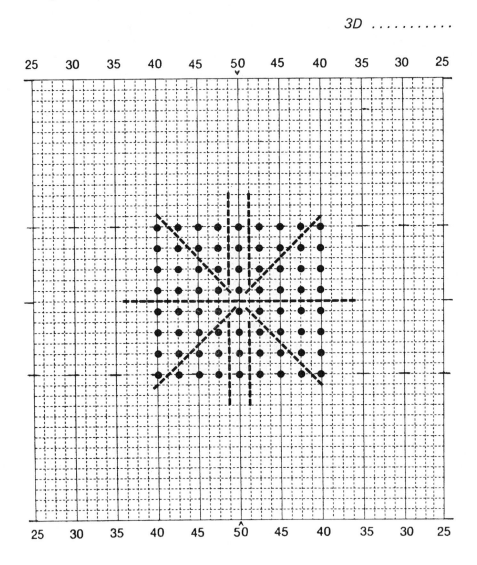

| 25 | 30 | 35 | 40 | 45 | 50 | 45 | 40 | 35 | 30 | 25 |

| 25 | 30 | 35 | 40 | 45 | 50 | 45 | 40 | 35 | 30 | 25 |

Logical Divisions—80 Players (8 x 10)

4D . . . .

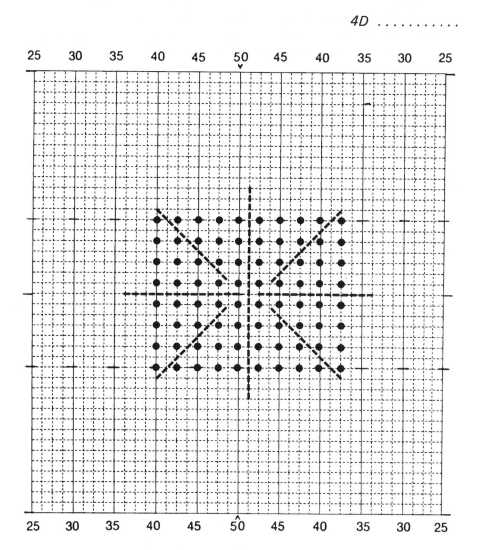

The number and extent of the variations that can be applied to this basic drill concept is limited only by the imagination and industry of the person designing the drill.

Block Band Drills

Another interesting variation allows the percussion rank to remain stationary, marking time on the 50 yard line throughout the entire drill. Leaving a rank stationary in the center provides very helpful guides to the bandsmen returning to the block position, but it does alter the appearance as shown in example 3E.

Block Band Drill No. 1E

Same Drill—Utilizing Stationary Percussion Rank

Using Division 3D—72 Players (8 x 9)

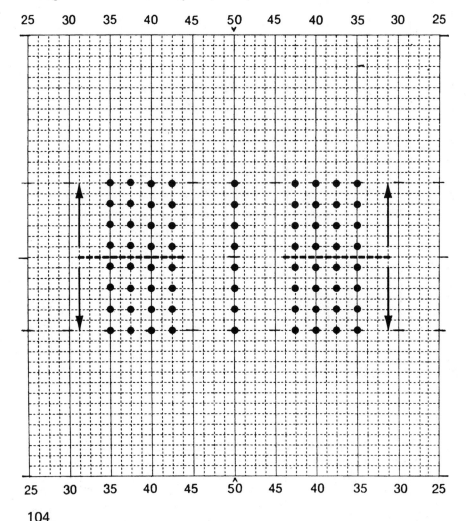

2E . . . .

3E . . . .

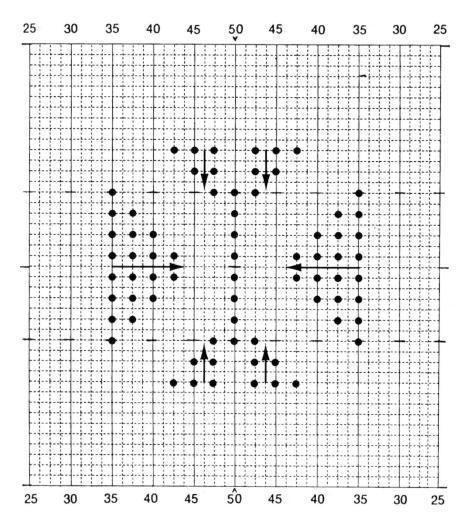

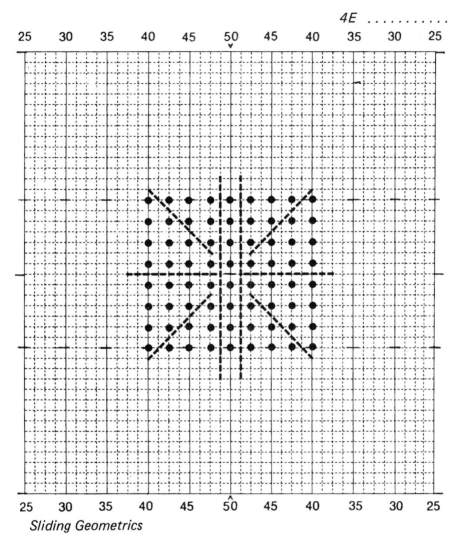

4E . . . .

25 30 35 40 45 50 45 40 35 30 25

Sliding Geometrics

There is another basic type of Block Band Drill which offers an interesting visual contrast to the previous drill and makes a good sequel to it. The Sliding Geometrics Drill requires the same basic fundamentals as the other Block Band Drills and is based on the principle which allows triangular segments of the block to "slide" past each other. They can do virtually any maneuvers as long as the wedges move at right angles to each other, or go in the same direction, creating constantly changing geometric patterns.

107

The following drill is an example of a fairly basic Sliding Geometrics routine, using 64 players, and based on a series of 16 count (or step) moves.

Begin by dividing the block into wedges, as nearly equal as possible, and assign to each large wedge a letter to identify it: A, B, C, or D, as shown in example 1F.

Sliding Geometrics Drill No. 1F

64 Players (8 x 8)

Example 2F—(the band is facing to the reader's left)
1. A & B: FM 16.
    C & D: RF 16 (Spin Turn for more flash).

2F . . . .

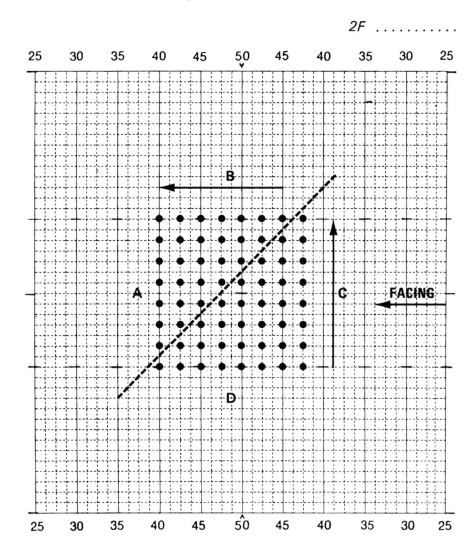

| 25 | 30 | 35 | 40 | 45 | 50 | 45 | 40 | 35 | 30 | 25 |

Example 3F
  2. A & B: TR 16.
      C & D: TR 16.

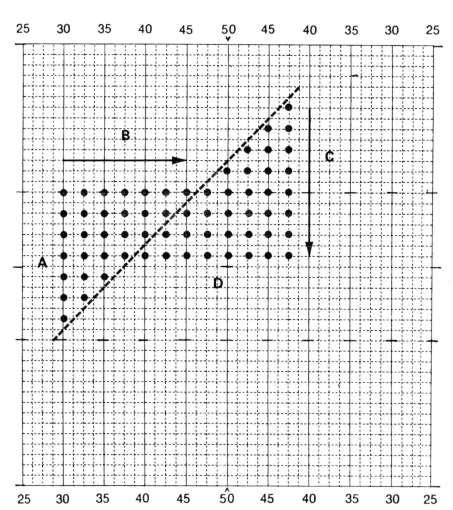

Example 4F

3. A: LF 16.
 B: FM 16.
 C: FM 16.
 D: RF 16 (Spin Turn).

4F . . . .

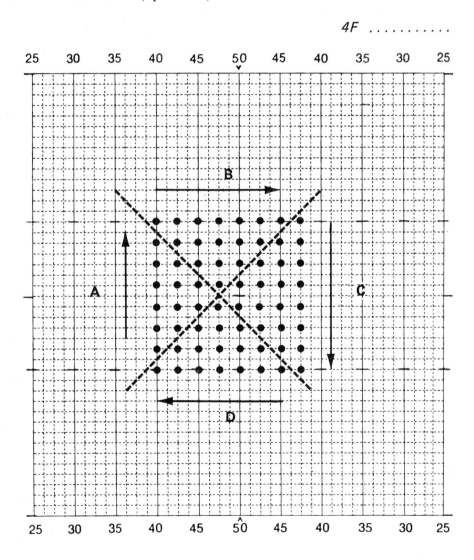

Example 5F—(This shows the Geometrics [of #4] after 8 counts).

5F . . . .

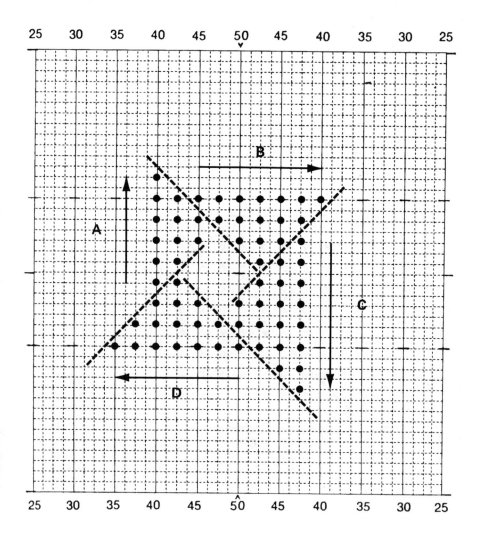

Example 6F
    4. A: TR 16.
        B: RF 16 (Spin Turn).
        C: LF 16.
        D: TR 16.

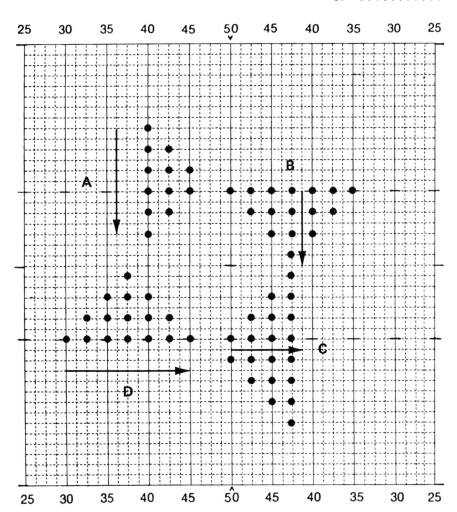

Example 7F

    5. A: LF 16.
          B: TR 16.
          C: LF 16.
          D: FM 16.

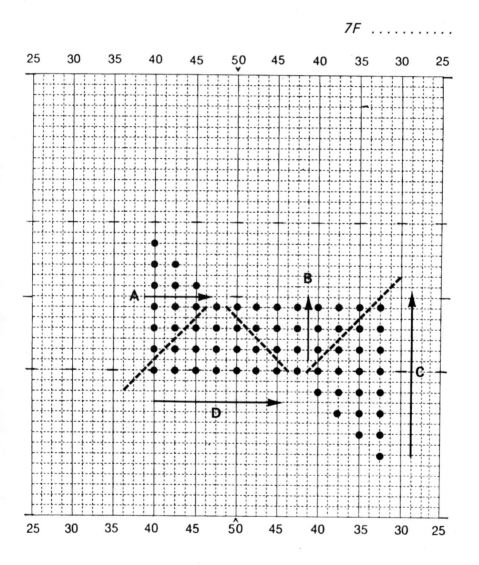

6. The band has now returned to the basic block (example 8F).

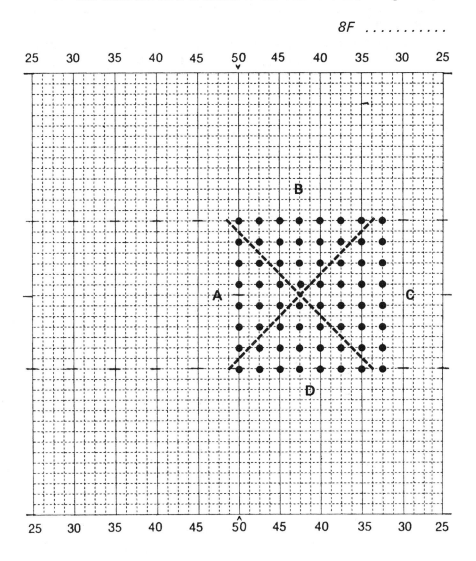

8F . . . .

As illustrated, this drill uses 5 moves of 16 counts each, or 80 counts. To lengthen this routine to 96 counts either return 16 steps (ten yards) back to the center of the field (A & B: TR 16; C & D:

LF 16); or add MT 8 twice, leaving a set pattern for 8 counts before making the next move, like holding the pattern shown in example 5F and in 6F.

Like the Block Band Drill discussed earlier, the extent to which this drill concept can be developed is limited only by the imagination and the creativity of the person designing or directing the drill.

Sliding Geometric Variation

Another interesting visual effect is created using the same (sliding geometrics) principles by "dropping out" a group of diagonal lines as the rest of the band continues marching downfield.

Sliding Geometrics Drill No. 1G

Block Band—64 Players (8 x 8)
   1. A: FM 16.
       B: RF 16.

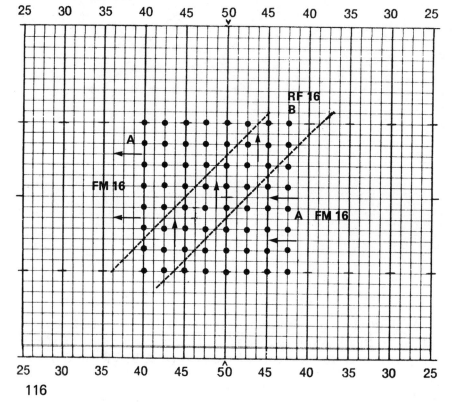

Example 2G
Position at end of 1st 8 counts.

2G . . . .

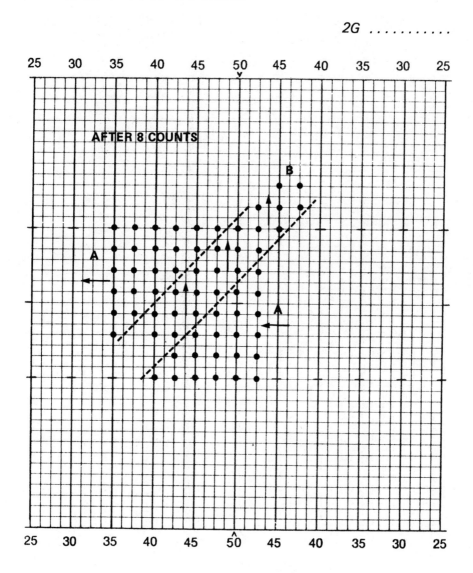

Example 3G
   2. All: TR 16.

3G . . . .

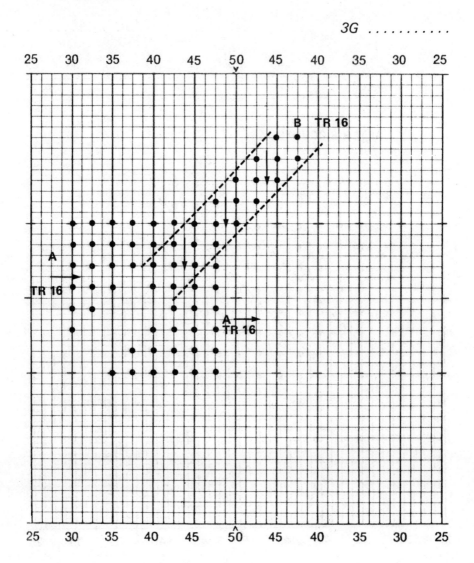

Example 4G
   3. All: FM 16.

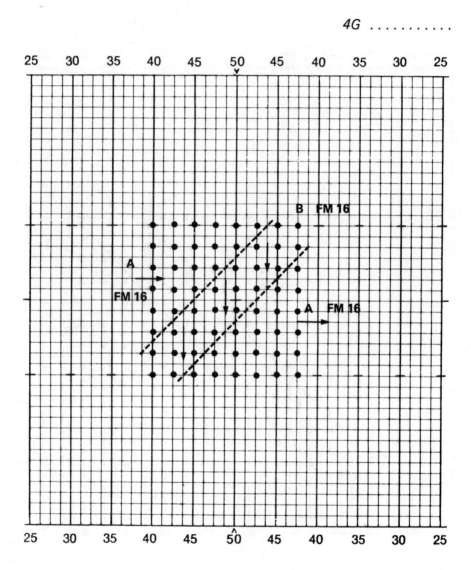

4G ....

119

Example 5G
   4. All: TR 16.

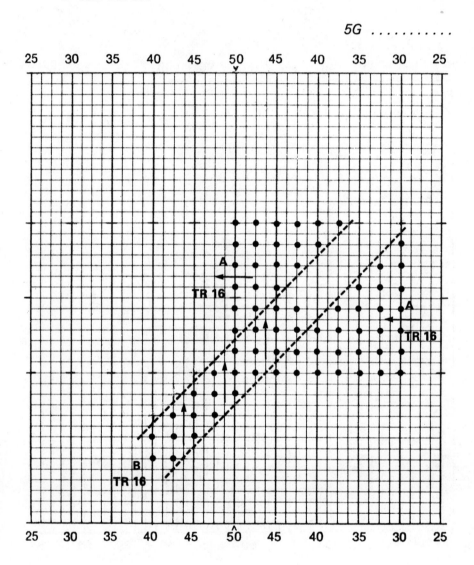

This is a nice 64 count drill which may be used in combination with the other block band drills. The completion of the last 16 counts returns everyone to their original block band position.

120

X and O Drills

One other basic Block Band Drill that provides an effective contrast to the drill concepts already explained is the "X" and "O" Drill. This drill is based on the same "sliding" principle as the Sliding Geometrics, but rather than keeping the band in tightly spaced wedges, this move expands the band into a larger unit spaced at larger intervals. Once again, these routines can be very satisfactorily performed using only three fundamentals: Forward March; Left or Right Flank; and To the Rear.

The basic rules applying to designing these drills are:

1. Every second person from left to right, and from front to rear is designated either an X or an O (see example 1H).

2. The Xs and Os may then move independently from each other, as long as they move either in the same direction, or at right angles to each other. (In the first illustration, 1H, all Xs will march forward 16 steps, while all Os will Right Flank 16 steps. It might appear at first glance that the Xs and Os are then on a collision course. However, on closer examination, it is clear that in four steps, when an O has reached the position where the next X was just standing, he has reached a hole created by the absence of another O who is also moving to his right.)

The X and O Drill which is illustrated is a basic drill for 64 players. There are 8 moves in the drill, and each move takes 16 counts. (With a smaller band, Xs and Os can be effective using only 8 count moves; however, with larger bands it takes longer moves for the new patterns to emerge successfully and be recognizable to the audience.)

Example 1H—(The band is facing towards the reader's left.)
1. All Xs: FM 16.
   All Os: RF 16.

X and O Drill No. 1H

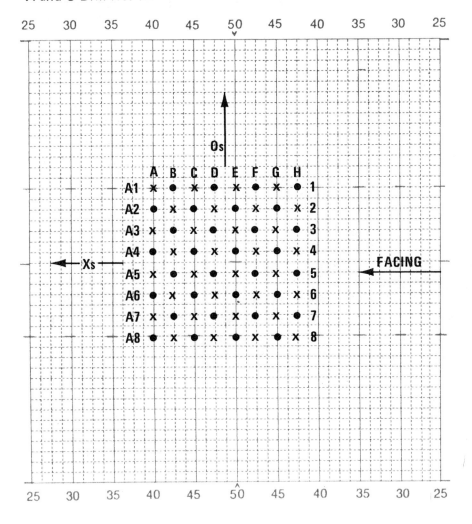

Example 2H
    2. All: TR 16.

2H . . . .

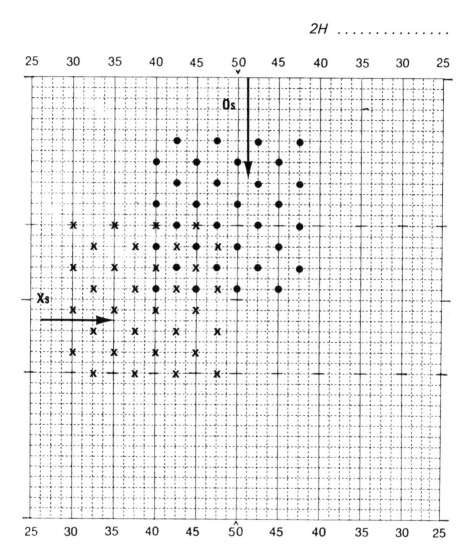

X and O Drills

Example 3H
   3. All: FM 16.

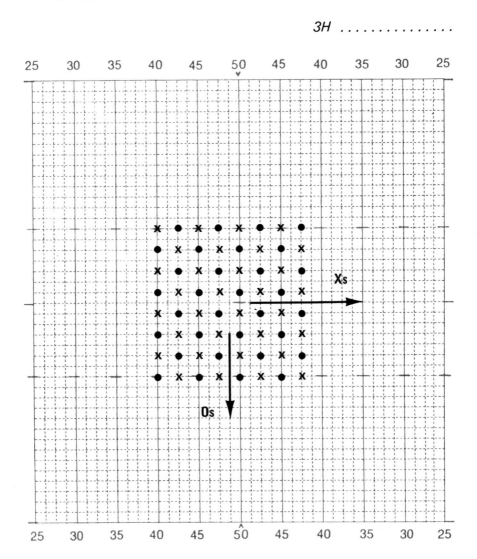

124

Example 4H
  4. All:TR 16.

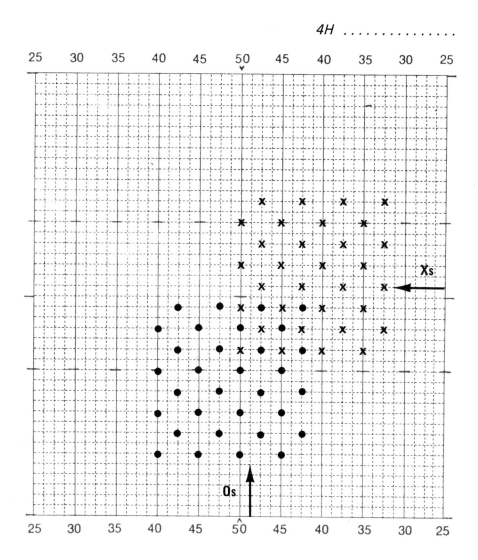

4H . . . .

X and O Drills

Example 5H

5. All 1-4 Os: FM 16.
    All 5-8 Os: TR 16.
    All A-D Xs: FM 16.
    All E-H Xs: TR 16.

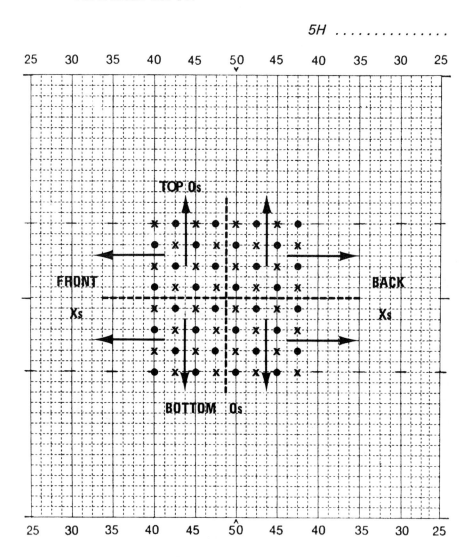

126

Example 6H
    6. A-D 1-4 Os: LF 16.
         E-H 1-4 Os: RF 16 (Spin Turn).
         A-D 5-8 Os: RF 16 (Spin Turn).
         E-H 5-8 Os: LF 16.
         A-D 1-4 Xs: RF 16 (Spin Turn).
         A-D 5-8 Xs: LF 16.
         E-H 1-4 Xs: LF 16.
         E-H 5-8 Xs: RF 16 (Spin Turn).

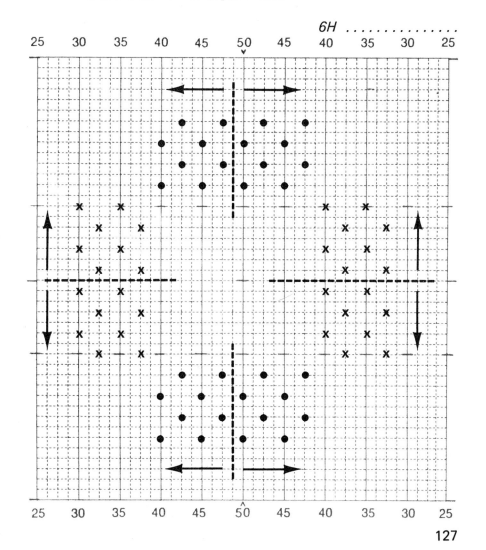

Example 7H

    7. Os A4, B3, C2, C4, D1, D3: TR 16.
        Os B5, C6, D5, D7: TR 16.
        Os E2, E4, F3, G4: TR 16.
        Os E6, E8, F5, F7, G6, H5: TR 16.
        All other Flank 16 or To the Rear 16 towards the center as shown on the chart.

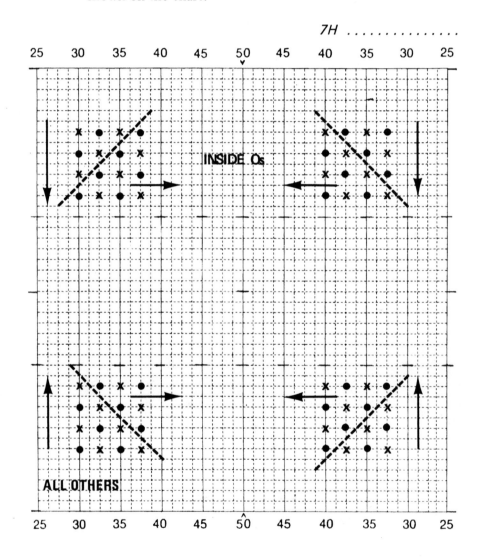

Example 8H

8. All Flank 16 towards center as shown.

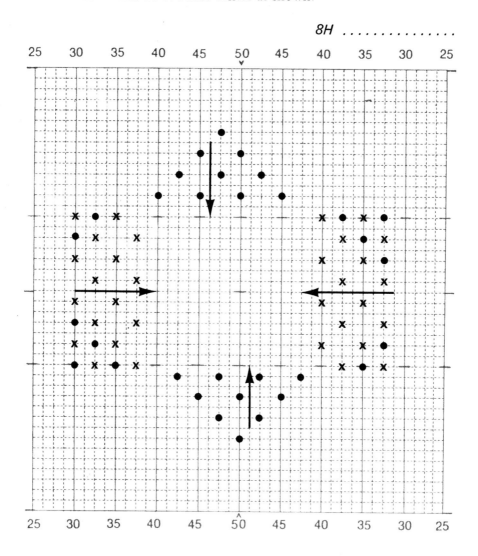

Example 9H
    (All players have now returned to their original starting position
    in the Block Band.)

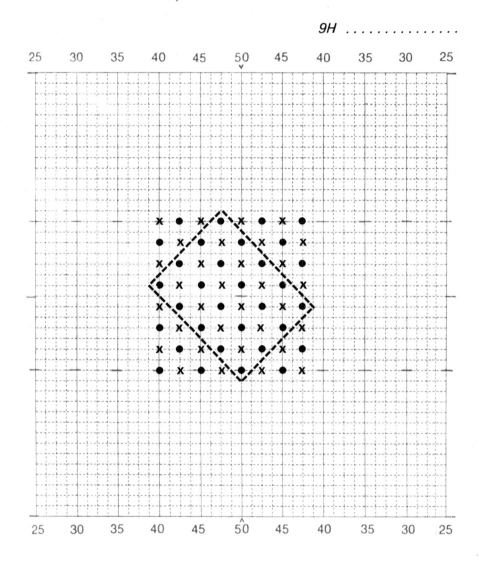

An X and O Drill in rehearsal.

An X and O Drill in performance.

Staging Devices

If there is need to create a staging formation to feature twirlers, flags, a kickline, or an instrumental soloist, example 6H, 7H, or 8H provides a very attractive staging design.

To use these for a stage, simply have the band Hit and Close and stand in one of those positions, facing the desired side of the stadium. At the conclusion of the feature, or solo, the band simply resumes motion completing the drill. If there is a visibility problem, i.e., seeing into the formation due to low bleachers, have the band kneel and continue playing in the feature formation. This is good show business even when visibility is excellent.

Expanding This Drill (to fit longer music)

A very effective and easy way to expand the illustrated drill, once the band has been divided into smaller segments (from example 6H to the end), is to move the band one half at a time. In other words, have half of the band MT 16 while the other half moves to its new position; then those who moved MT 16 while the other half moves. This can lengthen a drill considerably, and as was stated earlier it is a good safety device in that it gives all segments more time to think between moves, lessening the chance for errors.

Variations on This Theme

Once again, the variations that can be created using these basic principles are practically infinite. The basic division illustrated in example 5H could just as easily have been moved down the diagonals creating wedges instead of squares. From example 7H to the end, the drill could have been completed using any variations of Block Band Drills, or Xs and Os. The conclusion we used was simply a combination of both concepts.

Simple Block Band Drills, Sliding Geometrics, or X and O Drills may be used separately, or mixed together in numerous combinations. There are practically no limits on the interesting and ingenious variations and combinations that can be worked out using these principles. It is also interesting to combine them with other types of drills in order to create more variety in the visual appearance of the band. Some of the most useful types of drills to follow a Block Band sequence are those which utilize squads of four men who are at a two step interval from left to right, and a five yard interval from front to rear. The number of drill patterns which have been performed from this basic setup are enormous. We call these drills "Drills by Squads," and they are introduced in the next chapter.

Staging device achieved by stopping in an open position during drill.

8
Multiple Option
Drill Techniques II
Drills by Squads

Entire books have been written explaining and illustrating great numbers of drills from a basic four man squad position. It is not our purpose to try to present more drills than anyone else in this area. Instead, we want to present these concepts so they are clearly understood and can work logically with other popular types of drills. This will enable the marching band teacher to adapt these concepts and to create new and interesting drills to fit the individual needs of the band and the music to be performed.

Drills by Squads

In order to Drill by Squads, the interval between players in the squad must be ½ the distance between persons in the normal block, and the squads must be at least five yards apart (from front to back).

The necessary interval can be achieved from a block by having all even numbered ranks (B, D, F, H, etc.) march forward 4 steps, to the right of the person in front of them to a position halfway between the people on each side of them. With the band facing towards the reader's left, having even numbered ranks go to the right leaves all of the left hand pivots on the end, on the inserts marking, or "hash mark." This is an aid to better alignment.

Everyone should now be in the position shown in example 2I. Now, beginning at the right end of each new rank of 16 persons, "count-off" from the right, giving everyone a number from 1 to 4. This divides each line into four 4-man squads. For the move "L/S 8," the number 4 player is the pivot, and the other three persons in the squad revolve ¼ of a circle like the spokes of a wheel; the number 4 player turns in place with them and serves as the hub of the wheel.

A very simple basic Drill by Squads is illustrated:

Example 1I—(This begins from a starting position of a Block Band.)
1. Odd numbered ranks (A, C, E, G, etc.): MT 8.
    Even numbered ranks (B, D, F, H, etc.): FM 4 (to the R. of next player); MT 4.

Drill by Squads—64 Players (8 x 8) No. 1I

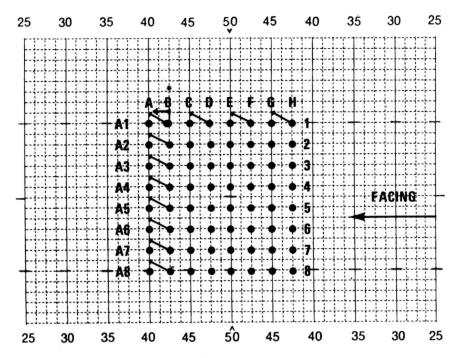

*For added flash have even-numbered ranks RF (spin turn) 2; MT 2; LF 4; or you could LF 2; MT 2; RF (spin turn) 4, but every other person would then be on the left side of the person who was previously in front of him or her.

136

Example 21

    2. All: L/S 8 (Number 1 players go to a point ¾ the way to the next line;

                Number 2s go exactly ½ the distance to the next line;

                Number 3s go ¼ the distance, and,

                Number 4s are the pivot, turning in place.)

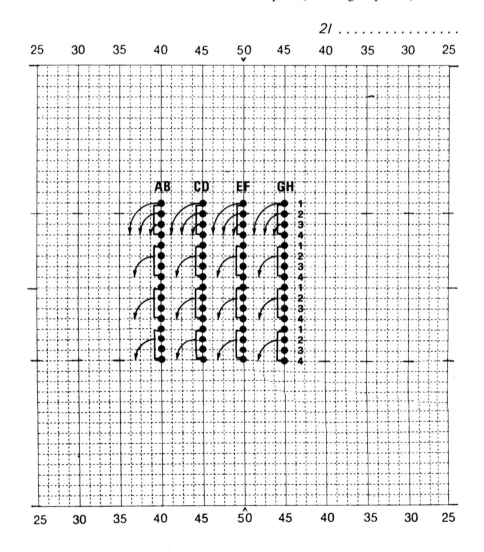

Example 3l

3. AB & CD: TR, R/S 8: (The TR takes place on the Right foot on the count of 8 of move #2, or on 4th beep of the preparatory 4 whistles if you are teaching these 8 counts at a time. [Like, "Beep, Beep, Beep, Turn, Go, 2, 3, 4, 5, 6, 7, 8].") By moving one-half of the band at a time and leaving the other half stationary, you lessen the problem of diminishing the tone quality of the band during manuever execution.

All others: MT 8.

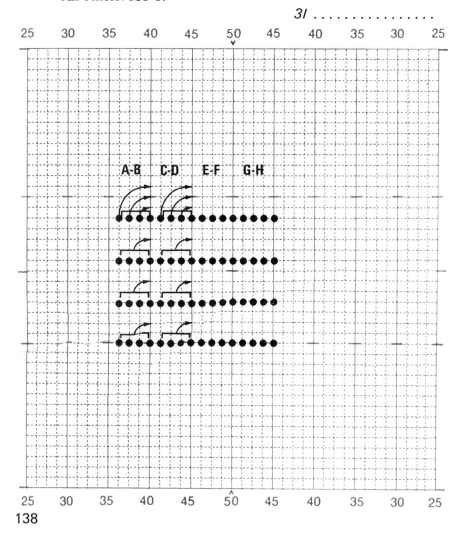

3l . . . .

Example 41
   4. AB & CD: MT 8.
      All others: TR, R/S 8.

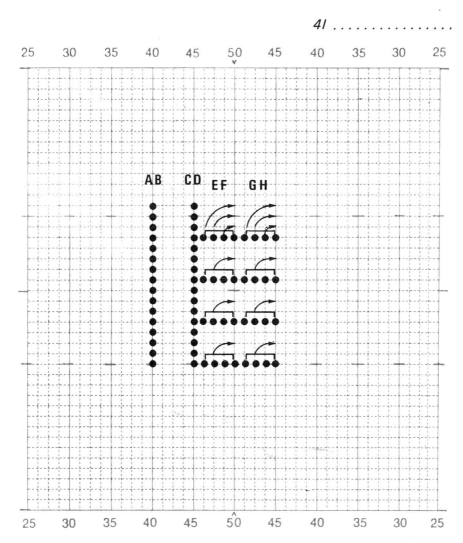

Example 51—(This shows the position after 32 counts [4 sets of 8].)
    5. AB & CD 1, 2, 7, & 8: TR, L/S 8.
           AB & CD 3, 4, 5, & 6: TR 8.
           EF & GH 1, 2, 7, & 8: R/S 8.
           EF & GH 3, 4, 5, & 6: FM 8.

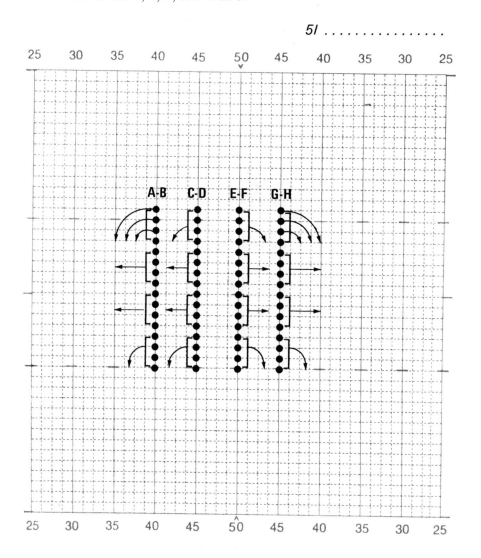

Example 61
    6. All 1, 2, 7, 8s: MT 8.
        AB & CD 3, 4, 5, & 6: L/S 8.
        EF & GH 3, 4, 5, & 6: R/S 8.

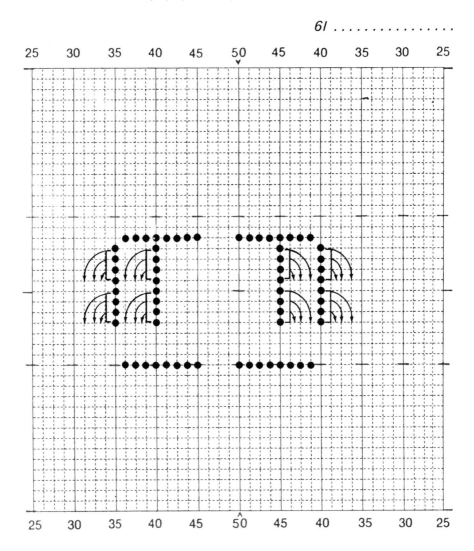

Example 71
    7. All AB & CDs: TR, R/S 8.
          All EF & GHs: TR, L/S 8.

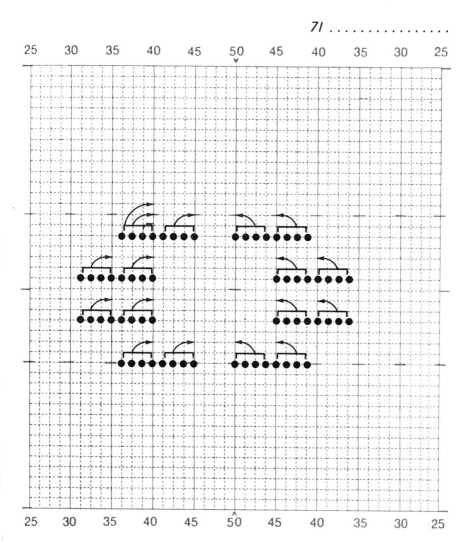

Example 8l
   8. All 1, 2, 7, & 8s: MT 8.
      All 3, 4, 5, & 6s: FM 8.

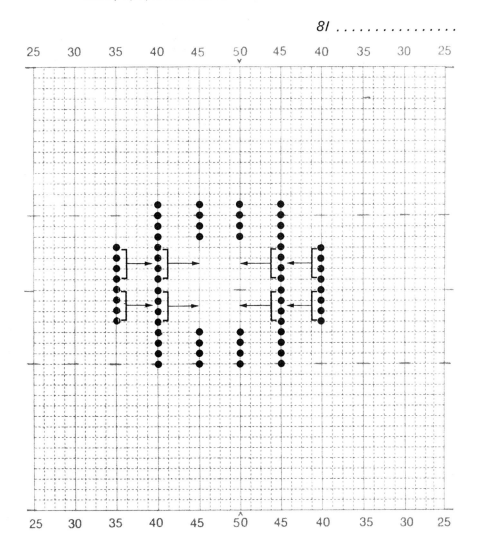

Example 91—(This shows the position after 64 counts.)

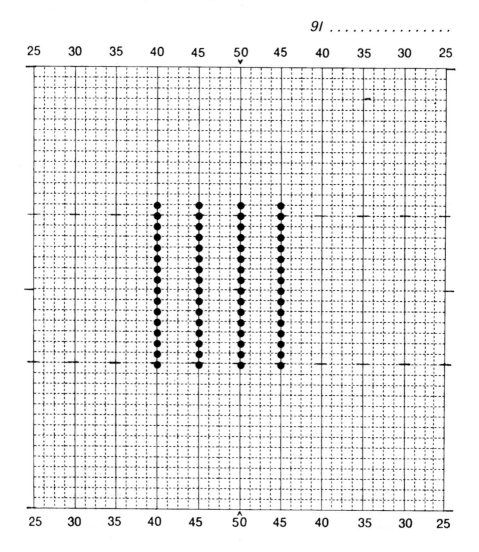

A drill by squads in actual performance.

Example 101—(This shows the next moves, if the goal is to continue into a basic concert formation.)
   9. All AB & CDs: R/S 8.
       All EF & GHs: TR, R/S 8.

101 . . . .

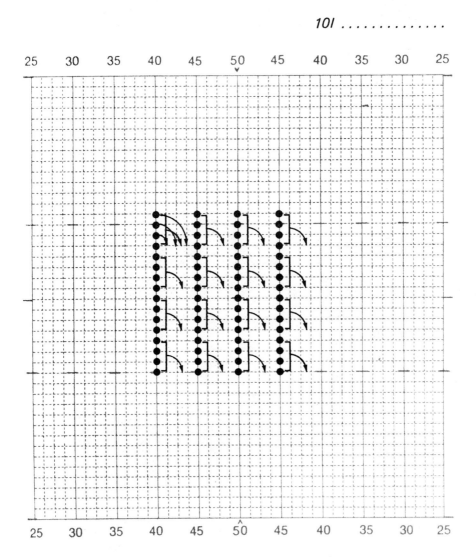

Example 11I
> 10. All 1, 2, and 7, 8s: FM 24: H & C.
>   All 3, 4, 5 & 6s: FM 16, MT 8, H & C.

11I . . . .

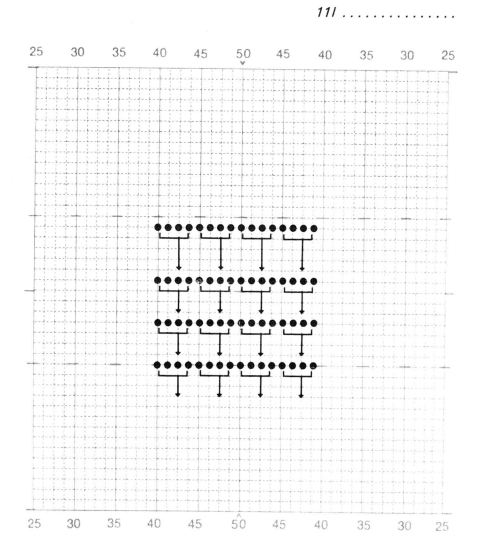

Example 121—(This shows the final concert formation, using an
  additional 32 counts to arrive in this position. This
  entire drill requires a total of 86 counts.)

121 . . . .

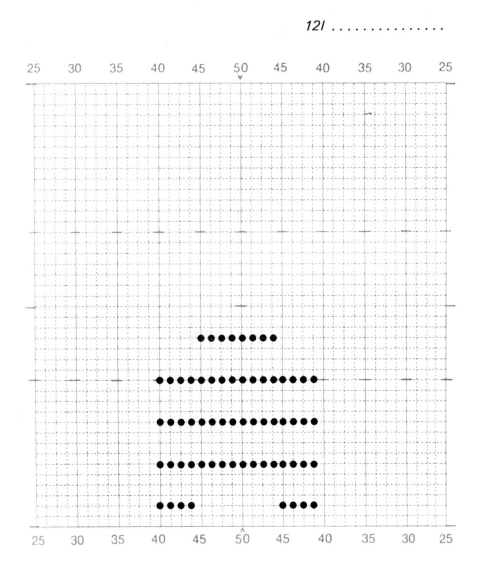

Basic concert formation

Staging Devices

In addition, there are opportunities within the illustrated drill where the band can face the bleachers, and either Hit and Close, or Mark Time, while twirlers, soloists, or whatever is desired are featured in the center. Two appropriate stopping places are shown on examples 6I and 7I.

Pinwheels (revolving four-squad groups)

Pinwheels can be set up from the basic formation in examples 2I or 9I, using only 8 counts.

149

Basic Pinwheels

Example 131—(Band is facing the reader's right.)
 1. AB 1, 2 & 5, 6: FM 8.
    EF 1, 2 & 5, 6: FM 8.
    AB 3, 4 & 7, 8: L/S 8 (Centered Pivot).
    EF 3, 4 & 7, 8: L/S 8 (Centered Pivot).
    CD 1, 2 & 5, 6: R/S 8 (Centered Pivot).
    GH 1, 2 & 5, 6: R/S 8 (Centered Pivot).
    CD & GH 3, 4 & 7, 8: MT 8.

131 . . . .
Setting Up Basic Pinwheels

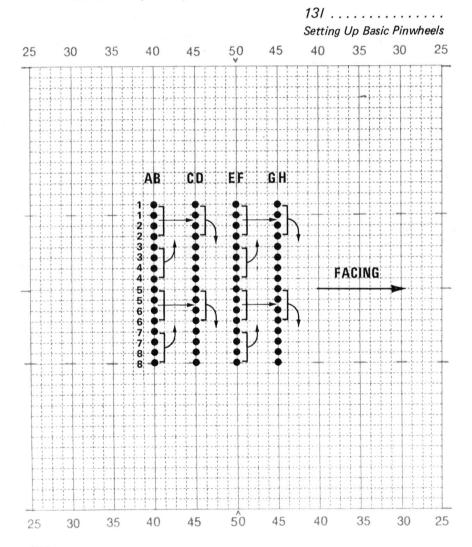

Example 141—(There are now 4 Pinwheels which can revolve as needed, each revolving around an imaginery pivot point on the yard line.)

141 . . . .

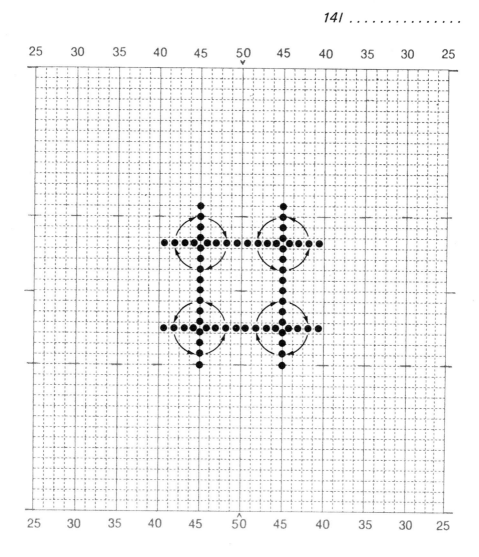

| 25 | 30 | 35 | 40 | 45 | 50 | 45 | 40 | 35 | 30 | 25 |

| 25 | 30 | 35 | 40 | 45 | 50 | 45 | 40 | 35 | 30 | 25 |

Basic Pinwheels

Another basic way to set four squad pinwheels using centered pivot squad moves is illustrated in examples 15I, 16I, 17I, and 18I. This takes 24 counts (three 8-count moves).

15I . . . .

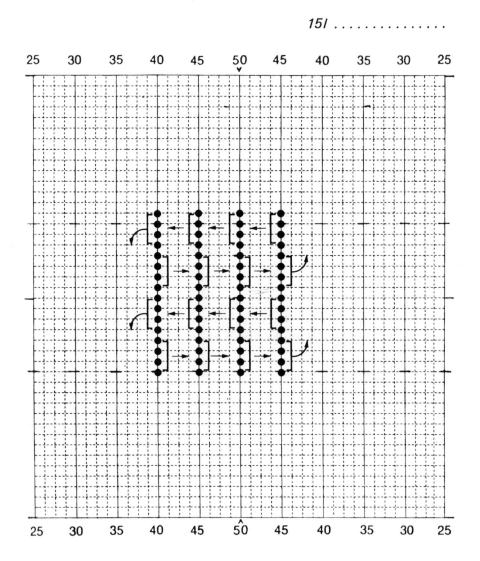

16l . . . .

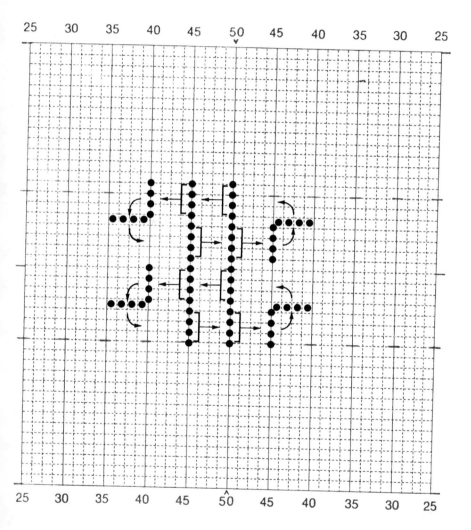

171 . . . .

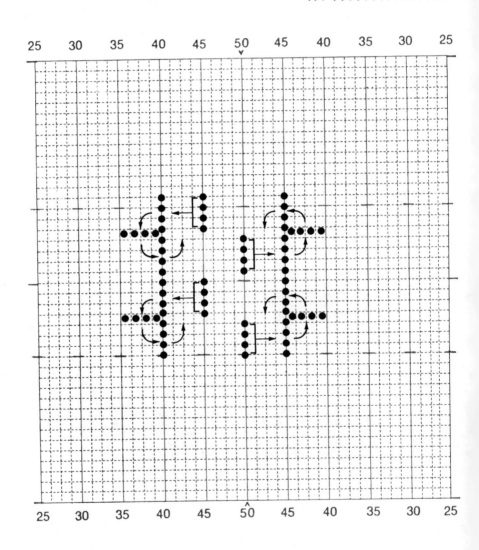

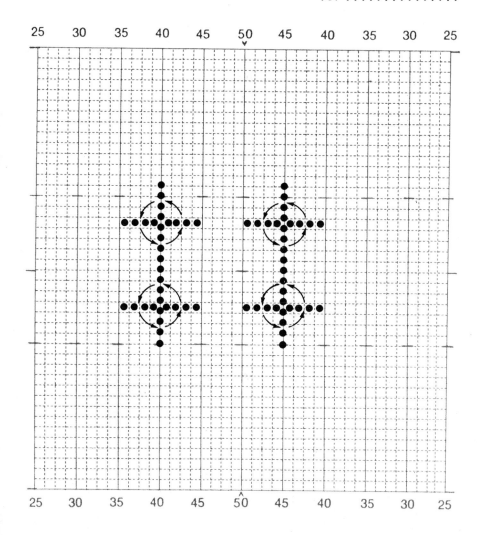

Drills by Squads (Opening Sequence)

The following is a very basic Opening or Downfield Sequence which utilizes only forward march and left by squads. Each squad will revolve one full revolution (360 degrees), or left by squads 8—four times, or 32 counts. Begin with lines ten yards apart.

Example 1J

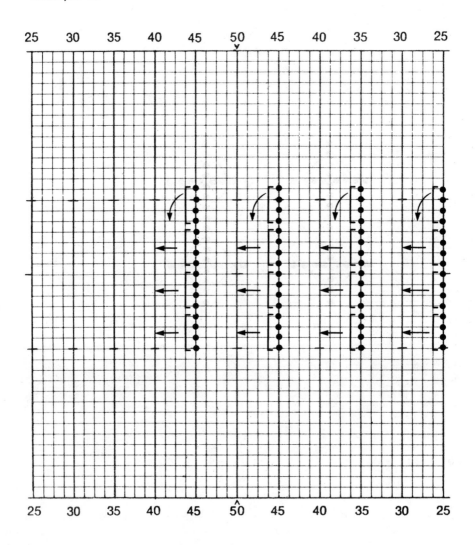

2J . . . .

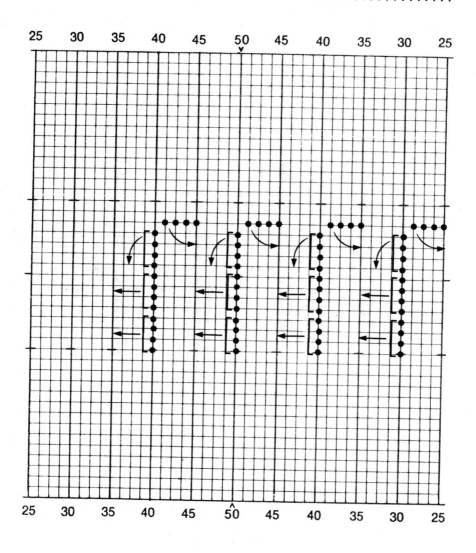

3J . . . .

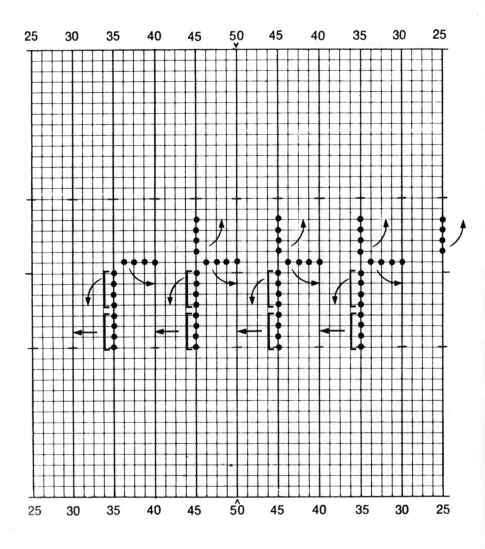

4J . . . .

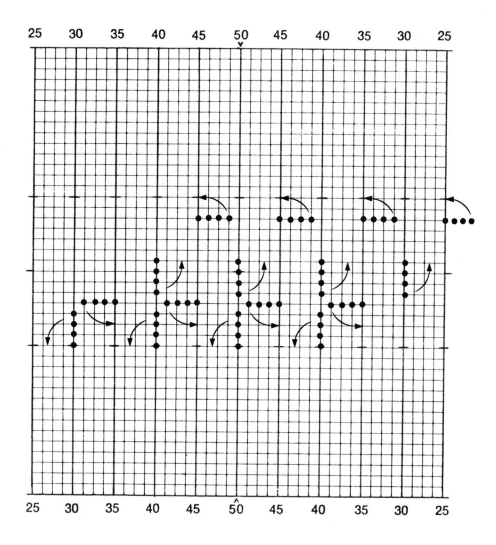

5J . . . .

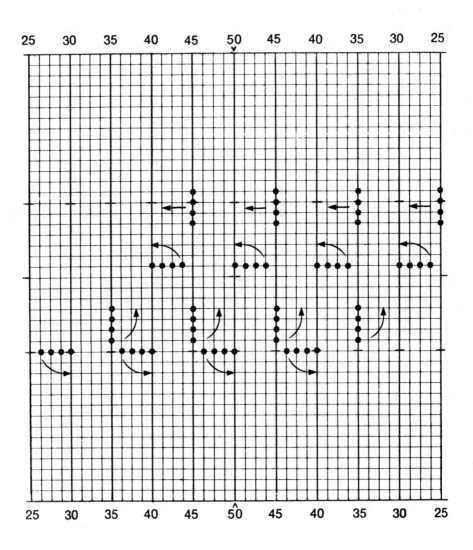

6J . . . .

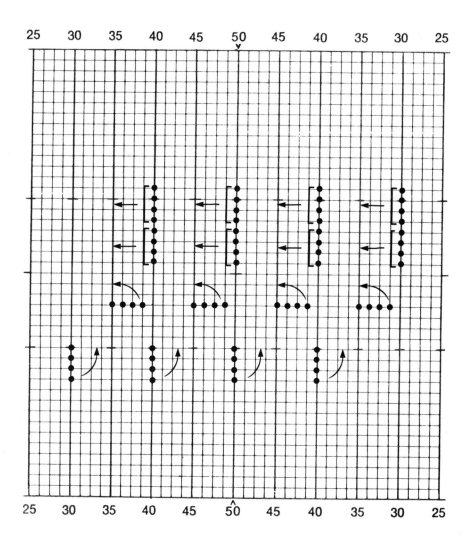

7J . . . .

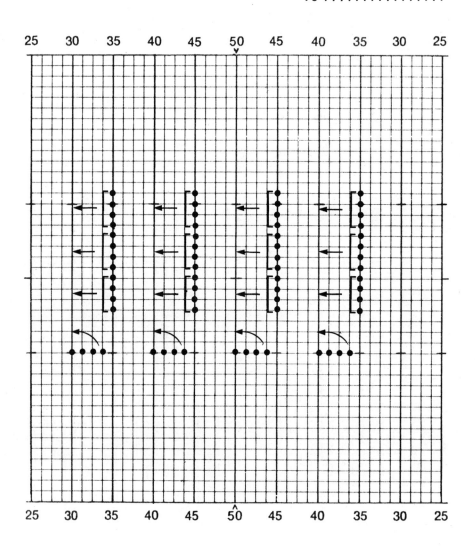

8J . . . .

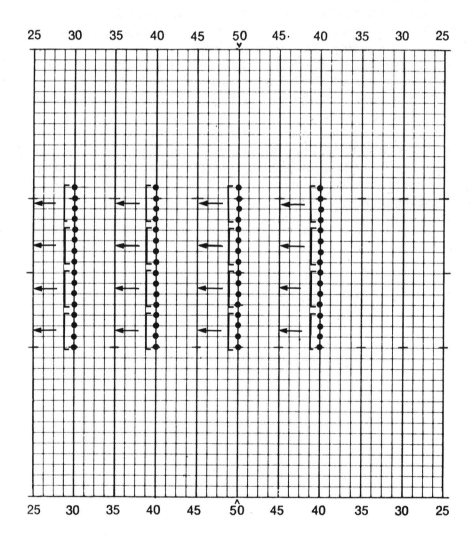

Variations of this Theme

Once again, these are extremely basic drills designed to illustrate the basic drill principles. They are not intended to illustrate exhaustive development of these concepts, but are, hopefully, a starting point from which any director may create appropriate drills and maneuvers for his own band using the music of his choice.

In order to utilize drills and staging formations illustrated in some other systems of precision marching, the basic interval between double ranks of squads (AB, CD, etc.) must be ten yards. This allows freer use of 4 squad pinwheels revolving on Centered Pivots.

By using the guidelines established for these drills it is possible for a director to take advantage of and adapt to his own group virtually every new marching concept which has been developed and widely used in the last several decades. Again, these are not limiting concepts, but rather, broadening concepts. The only limitation on the extent to which these concepts may be expanded and developed is the determination and creativity of the person working with them.

9
Multiple Option
Drill Techniques III
Step-twos

Step-two drills have been one of the standard devices utilized by good drill bands for many years.

They are easy to teach, and they can provide a seemingly endless variety of different patterns and designs. The drills which will be shown will use lines of 32 persons standing two 22½ inch steps apart. One of the nice features of these drills is their flexibility and adaptability, as they can be used with virtually any size band.

Basic Step-two Devices or Drills

There are two ways to get from the position shown in example 1K to the position shown in example 2K or 3K:

  1. Traditional Step-twos: Marchers 16 and 17: FM

                                              15 and 18: MT 2; FM

                                              14 and 19: MT 4; FM

                                                13 and 20: MT 6; FM

                                              etc. until all are off the line

2. By Dropping Off every two counts:
   Marchers 1 and 32: MT
   2 and 31: FM 2; MT
   3 and 30: FM 4; MT
   4 and 29: FM 6; MT
   5 and 28: FM 8; MT
   etc. until line is fully expanded

When used as an entry drill there is greater impact by having everyone step off at once and drop off, rather than mark time in place and then step off. This creates a much stronger feeling of immediate motion.

Example 1K

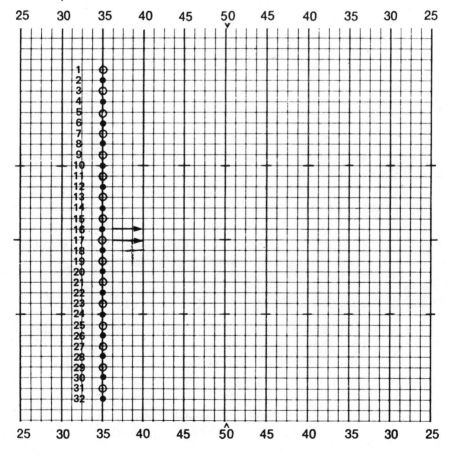

Example 2K—(After 30 counts).

2K . . . .

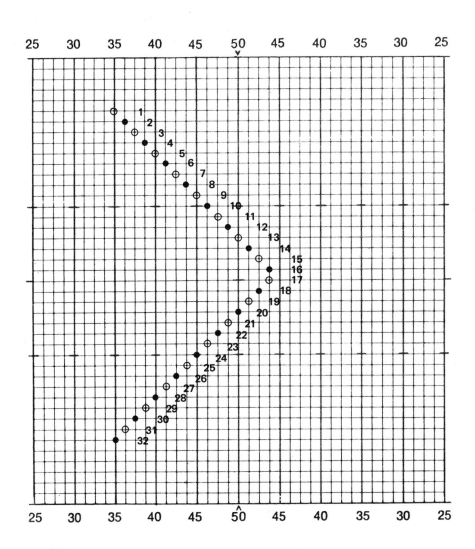

Basic Step-twos

It takes 30 counts to fully expand a line of 32 persons. Since it is important to start your next series of moves at the end of 8 counts, and the moves should be keyed to a yard line: 1) If you used step-twos (No. 1 above), adding two more counts will move your point people to the yard line; 2) If you want to Drop Off to this position, have everyone FM 2, and then start dropping off every two counts.

Example 3K—(After 32 counts).

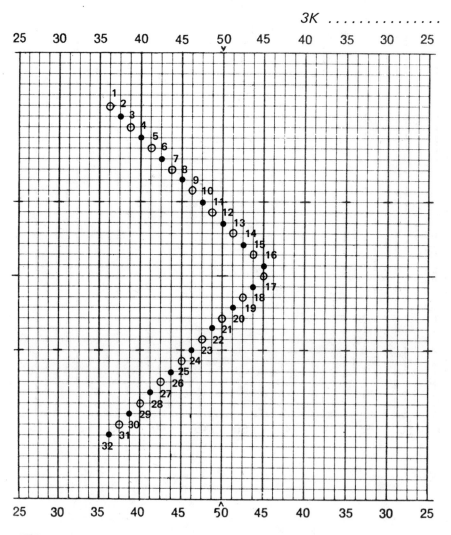

After 32 counts (example 3K) you again have several options as to what kind of move to add next. Three logical next moves are:

1. Pick-up from the rear. Marchers 1 and 32: FM
   2 and 31: MT 2; FM
   3 and 30: MT 4; FM
   4 and 29: MT 6; FM
   etc. until all are again in a single line

Example 4K—("Pick-up" after 8 counts).

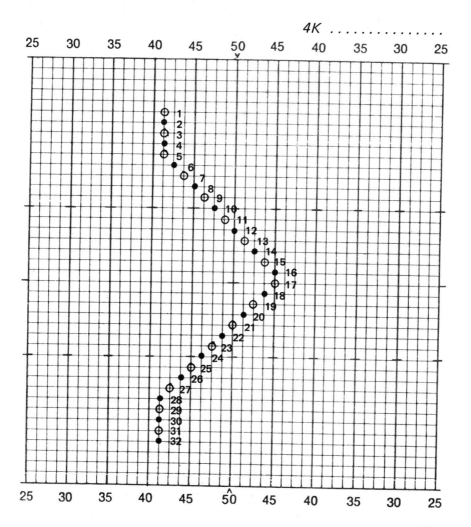

Example 5K—("Pick-up" after 16 counts).

5K . . . .

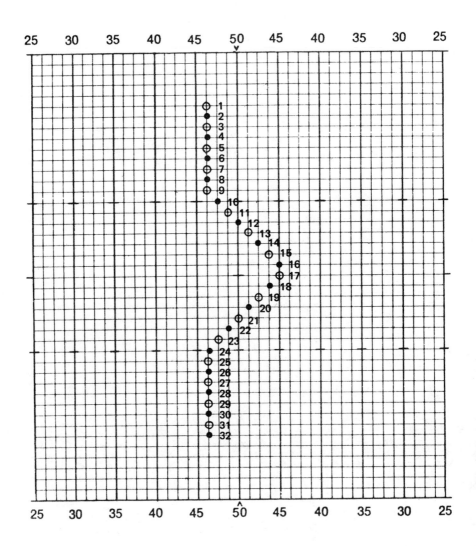

170

2. Stack-up on the line.   Marchers 16 and 17: MT
   15 and 18: FM 2; MT
   14 and 19: FM 4; MT
   13 and 20: FM 6; MT
   etc. until all are on the line

Example 6K—("Stack-up" after 8 counts).

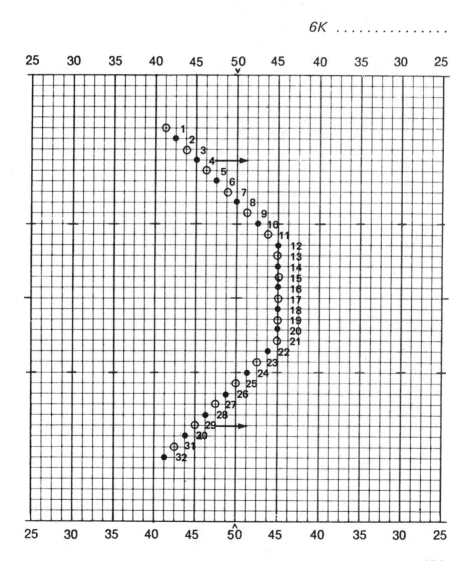

6K . . . .

3. Each TR when they hit the yard line.

Example 7K—(Each TR when they hit the yard line.)

7K . . . .

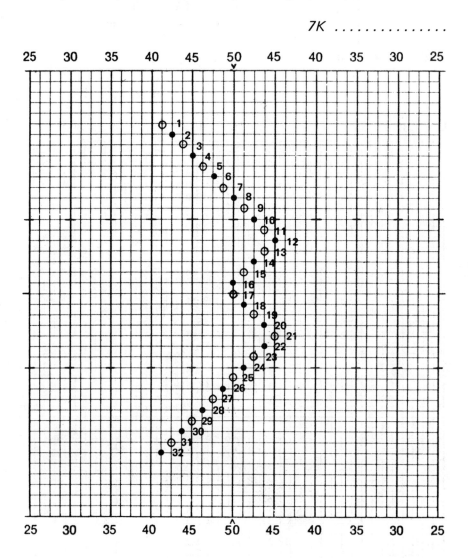

Note: Step-twos do not have to begin with the center persons. They may be started from either end or both ends, or from any point in between.

172

Step-twos into Diamonds and Changing Parallelograms

One of the most popular and fascinating uses of progressive movements is illustrated in the next series of diagrams.

It is possible to form the diamond shown in example 1L by moving the entire line forward from the 40 yard line with every other person dropping off in the position indicated. This would take 32 counts.

It could also be formed from two lines of 16 players each, marching toward each other from both 40 yard lines. This takes 16 counts.

Probably the most effective way to form the diamond is the 16 count move shown on chart 1L, first 16 counts.

1L . . . .

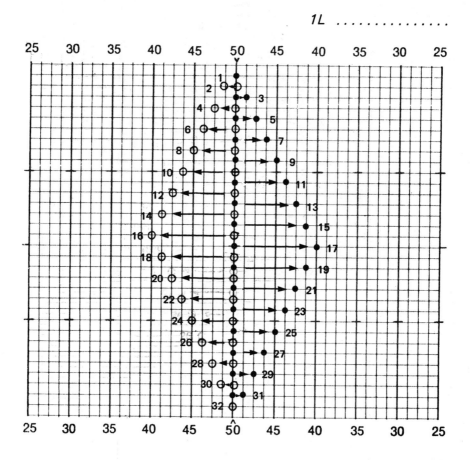

Basic Step-twos

From this position everyone marches 16 steps as shown on the chart, in the direction indicated by the arrow, executing TR on the 40 yard line.

Example 2L — (Second 16 counts)   *2L* . . . .
          FM as shown.
          TR on 40 yard lines.

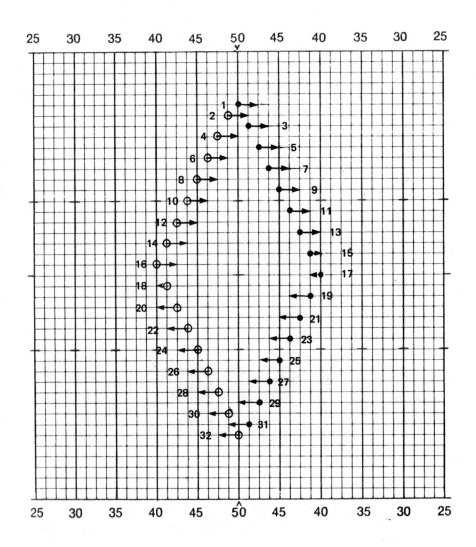

Example 3L — (After 8 counts).

3L . . . .

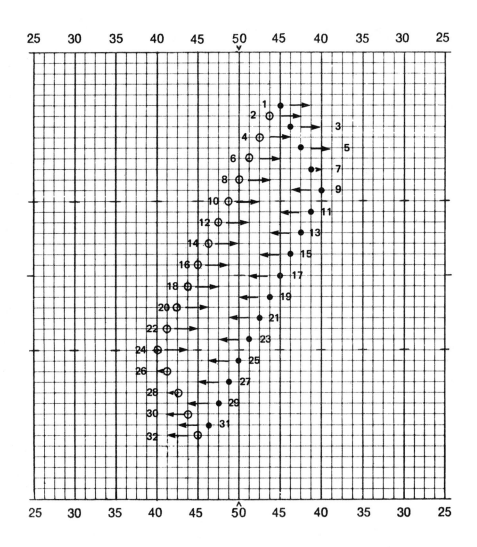

Example 4L — (After 16 counts).   4L . . . .

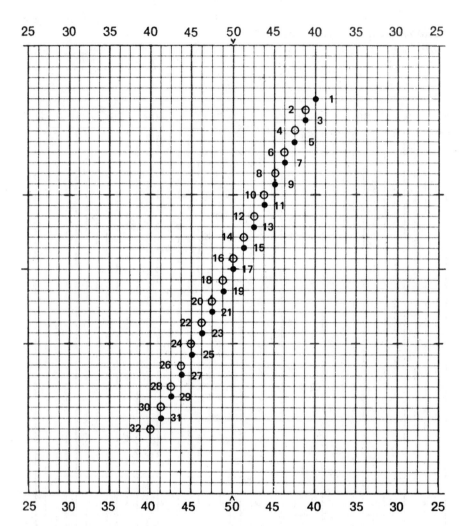

Three options from this point are:
1. all continue 16, returning to ◊ , with the sides reversed.
2. or all to the rear 16 which reverses the pattern back to the original ◊.
3. or divide in the center (1-16, 17-32) and make two ◊'s each using 16 persons.

Drills which are rigidly keyed to the yardlines (like Block Band Drills or Drills by Squads) are among the safest and most secure types of drills to teach and perform since the students have so many "guides" to key off from. Most moves occur on or exactly halfway between yard lines, and most moves should fit the musical phrases in multiples of 8s and 16s. If your band is ready to attempt something daring and exciting, you have probably entertained the idea of doing Circle Drills. The next chapter introduces such drills. While they do not allow the student to have as many guide points on the field itself, they can be very effective—especially with a large band in a large stadium; and, again, if they are properly set up, and the band is fundamentally sound, they are not as difficult to teach as they might seem to be.

10
Multiple Option
Drill Techniques IV
Circle Drills

Probably no single drill idea has received so much attention in the late 1960s and 70s as Circle Drills and all the variations and deviations that have been evolved and devised from them. Once again, this chapter will not attempt to present every Circle Drill yet devised, or even attempt to suggest the numerous variations that are possible. Instead, it is our goal to explain how Circle Drills can be set up and taught by relatively inexperienced teachers to relatively inexperienced bands, and not necessarily large ones either. These are basic concepts which when mastered will allow the serious student of marching bands to devise and create Circle Drills which are appropriate for his band, for the music to be performed, and for the situation in which they will be presented.

Circle Drills

Circle Drills utilize concentric circles, adjacent circles which contract and expand against each other, and combinations of these two ideas. It is not a difficult problem to move from the Basic Block, or the half interval necessary for a Drill by Squads, to a Circle Drill, but the ranks (A, B, C, D, etc.) should be 10 yards apart before starting to form the circles. The following are examples of basic circle drills:

178

Example 1M—(If you begin in a block, first move the even ranks forward four steps, stopping in a position halfway between the person who was in front and the person on his right. Marchers should now be at a 2-step interval—5 yards apart.)

1. AB: FM 8; MT 8.
   CD: MT 16.
   EF: TR, MT 8; FM 8.
   GH: TR 16.

Basic Circle Drills   *1M* . . . .

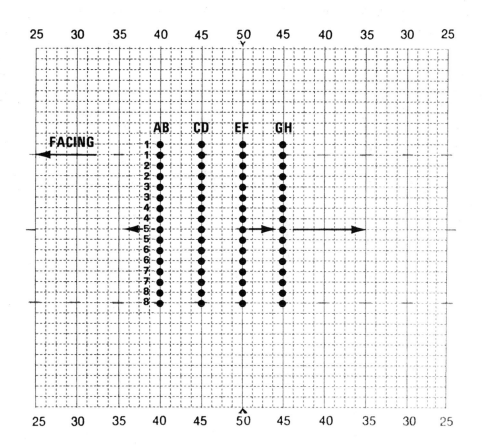

Example 2M

 2.   AB: TR 8.
 CD 1, 2: TR, R/S 8.
 CD 3, 4, 5, 6: TR, MT 8.
 CD 7, 8: TR, L/S 8.
 EF 1, 2: TR L/S 8.
 EF 3, 4, 5, 6: TR, MT 8.
 EF 7, 8: TR, R/S 8.
 GH: TR 8.

to Concentric Circles   2M . . . .

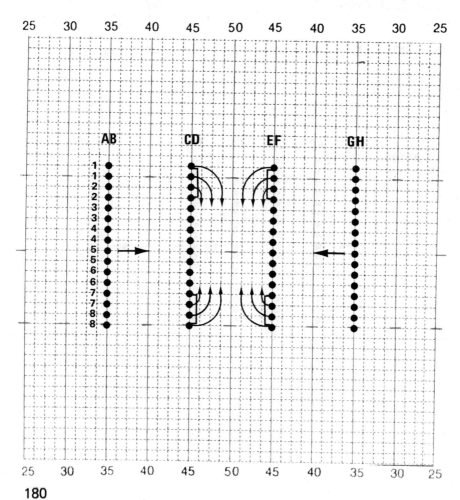

Example 3M
3. AB: FM 8.

CD and EF: Close to circle 8 (as indicated on chart facing the center of the circle.)

3M . . . .

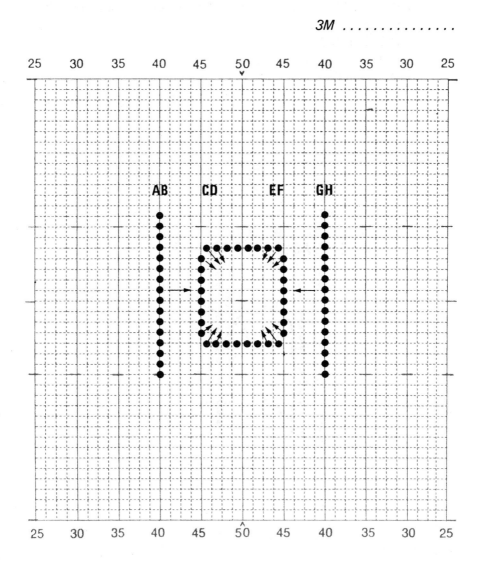

Example 4M
4. AB 1, 2: R/S 8.
    AB 3, 4, 5, 6: MT 8.
    AB 7, 8: L/S 8.
    CD, EF: TR 8 (facing outward, the exact opposite from the circle.)
    GH 1, 2: L/S 8.
    GH 3, 4, 5, 6: MT 8.
    GH 7, 8: R/S 8.

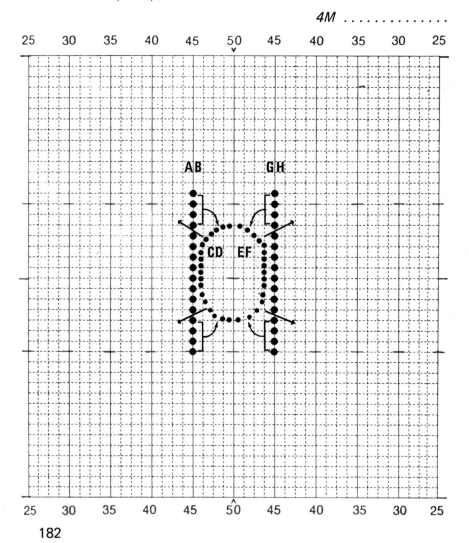

Example 5M
    5. CD, EF (the outside circle): FM 8.
          AB, GH (the inside box): Close to circle 8 (as shown on chart, facing the center of the circle.)

5M . . . .

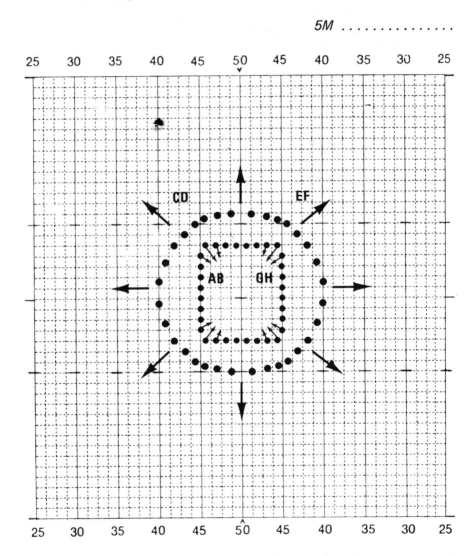

Example 6M—(You now have two concentric circles.)

    6. CD, EF (outside circle): FM 8 (continues expanding).

         AB, GH (inside circle): TR 8 (facing outward).

Note: The circles can pass through each other by instructing the outside circle to TR 16; and the inside circle to FM 16. To pass them through each other again, instruct both to TR 16. Also, the circles can revolve in opposite directions for another interesting effect.

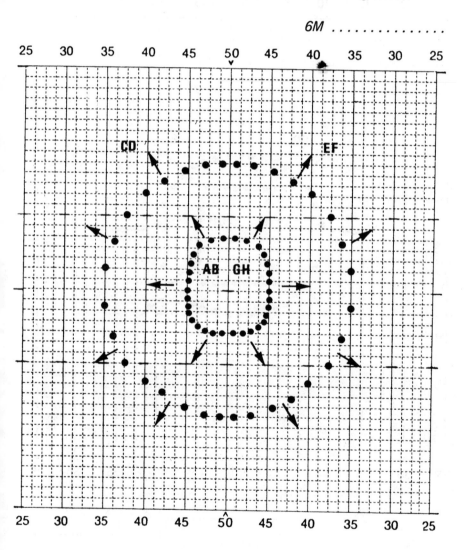

Concentric circles in actual performance.

Example 7M—(To form Adjacent Circles, again begin with ranks 10
yards apart.)
   7. All 1, 2s and 7, 8s: R or L/S 8 to form box.
       All others: MT 8.

to Adjacent Circles   *7M* . . . .

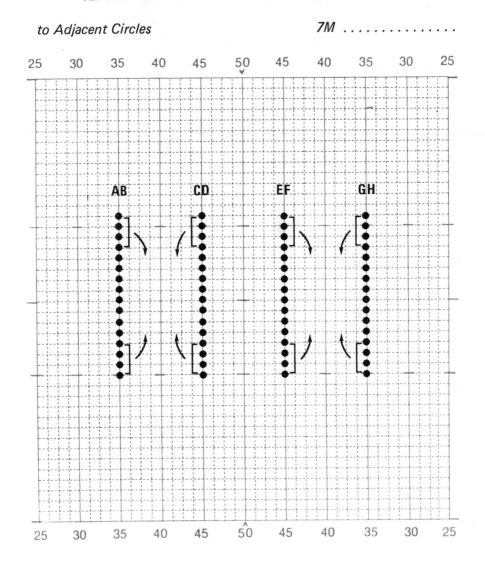

Example 8M

8. AB, CD: Flank or TR 6, MT 2 to the position shown in next example.

   EF, GH: Flank or TR 4, MT 4 to the position shown in next example.

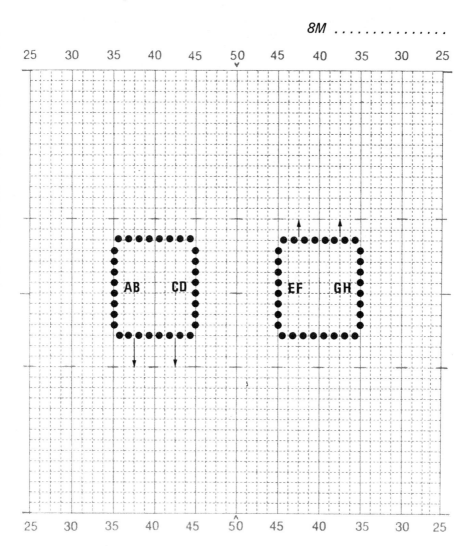

8M . . . .

Example 9M
 9. AB, CD: Close to Circle 8 (facing center of circle).
  EF, GH: MT 8.

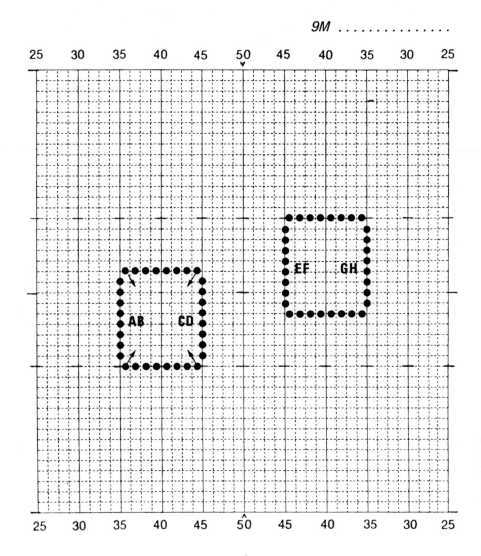

Example 10M

10. AB, CD: TR 8 (facing outward from center of circle).
    EF, GH: MT 8.

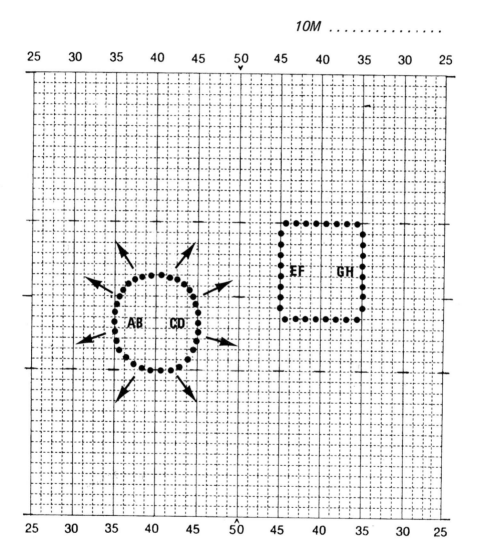

Example 11M

11. AB, CD: FM 8 (continuing to expand the circle).
     EF, GH: Close to circle 8 (facing center of circle).

11M . . . .

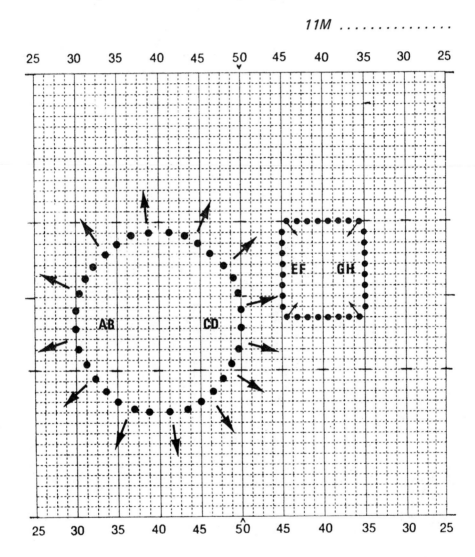

Example 12M
  12. All: TR 8.

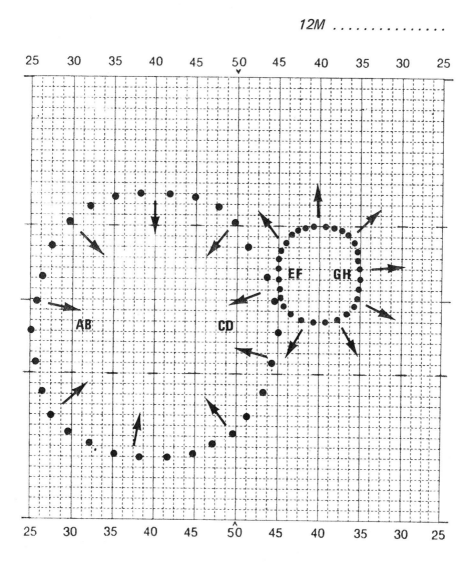

12M ....

5-photo sequence showing development of Adjacent Circle Drill

Example 13M
  13. All: FM 8.
Note: To contine the illusion of contraction and expansion, have All TR 16, and TR 16 as long as you wish the illusion to continue. Again, it can be interesting to have each circle revolve, one clockwise, and one counterclockwise; this results in an effect similar to meshing gears, or adjacent wheels.

13M . . . .

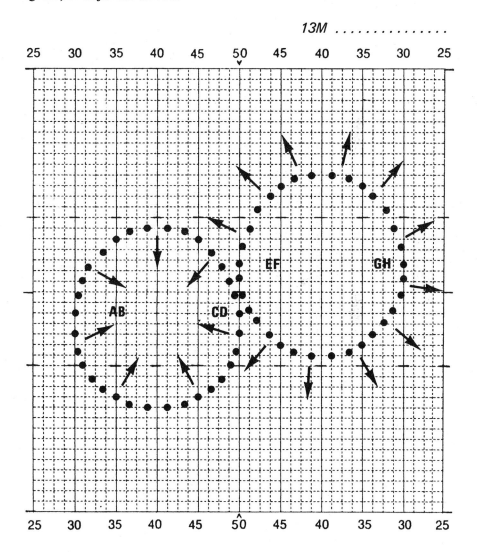

More Circles

Another approach to setting up circles is illustrated in the following examples. This set-up allows the concentric circles to be set at a five yard interval.

Example 1

1. Basic set-up.

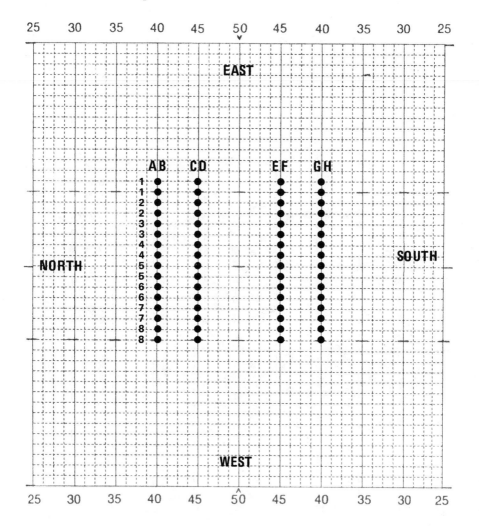

Example 2
2. AB & GH 1-4, and CD & EF 5-8: Flank (face and either march, or mark time) East to the position indicated on next illustration. AB & GH 5-8 and CD & EF 1-4: Flank West to next position.

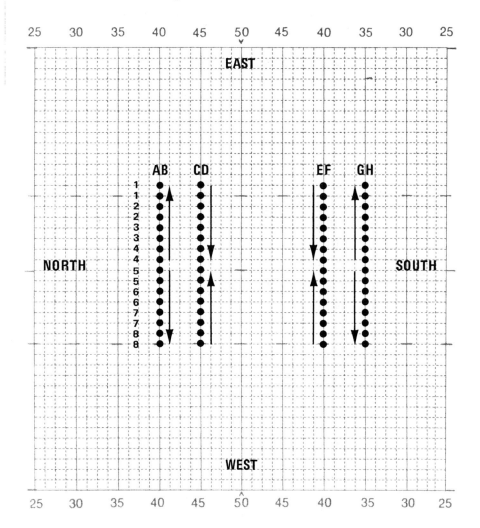

Circle Drills

Example 3

3. Move to this position (evenly spaced).

or,

Move to this optional set-up, with ends of lines grouped to be nearer their stopping position in the circles.

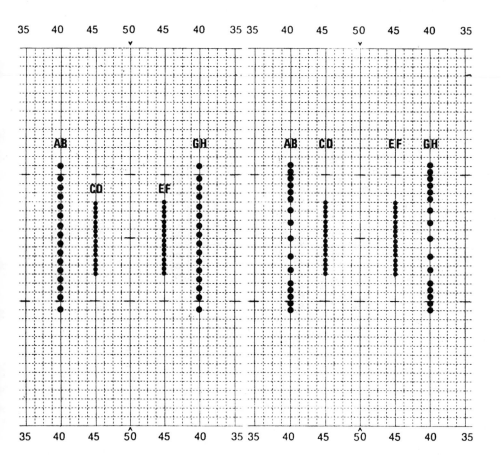

198

Example 4

4. All face the center, and FM (or execute Flank movement) towards the center, forming the indicated circle (example 5).

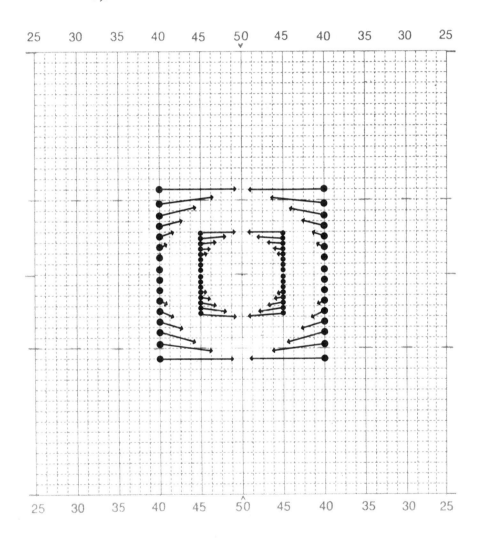

Example 5

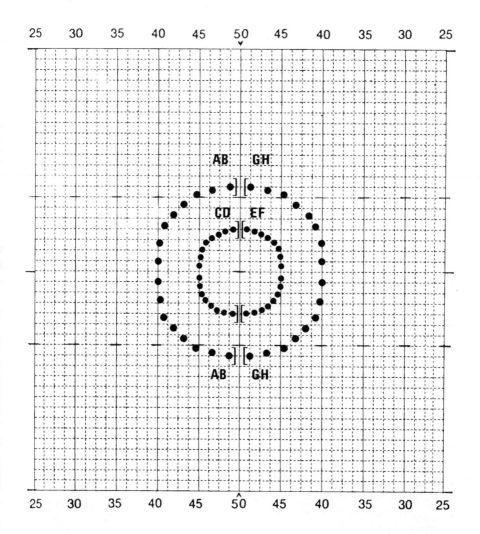

Circle Variations

By combining circles into double circles (2 circles of 32 players becomes 1 circle of 64 players, or 2 circles of 48 players [multiples of 12-person ranks rather than 8] become a single circle of 96), and utilizing progressive movements—Step-ones and Step-twos—a number of very appealing variations can be developed from the circles.

While these devices can be utilized with a single circle of 64 players, all of the patterns are actually more effective with larger size bands. A single circle of 96 (48 + 48) players is an ideal size for some of these moves, and 2 circles of 64 players (128) or 2 circles of 96 players is even more ideal. Also, it is important in these drills for all players to be spaced "evenly" around the circle.

To set up these drills, begin with the band in concentric circles as shown in illustration 5 on page 198. Have the outside circle Mark Time 8 while the inside circle marches outward 8 counts into the next circle. The new circle should now contain all 64 players, with one person from the inside circle between each two persons in the outside circle—so they are now "every-other" person.

In example 1, the players move from a single circle of 64 players to a four petal flower. The point persons in the circle remain stationary, marking time as everyone else moves forward toward the center. As in the Step-one or Step-two illustrations discussed earlier, the players can either all Forward March toward the center at once, dropping off in the indicated position; or they can literally "Step 1" leaving the circle on each consecutive count, and all arrive at the position at the same time.

Example 1—(64 Players)
Flower Petals—1-step interval (Step-ones)

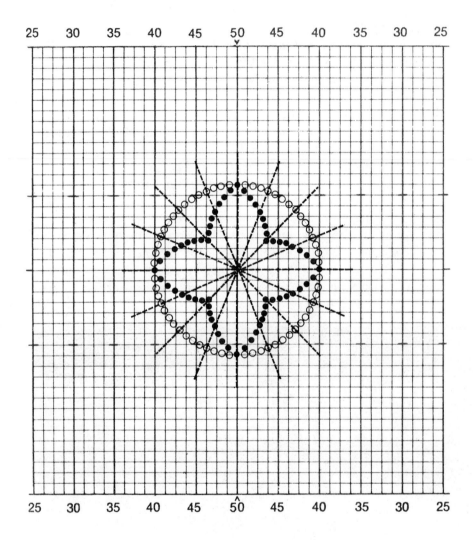

Example 2 shows the same type of pattern by a 64-piece band, but this time the circle is 10 yards wider (from the 35 to the 35), and the petals are in a two-step interval, so they are arrived at every two steps rather than every step (Step-twos).

Example 2—(64 Players)
Flower Petals—2-step interval (Step-twos)

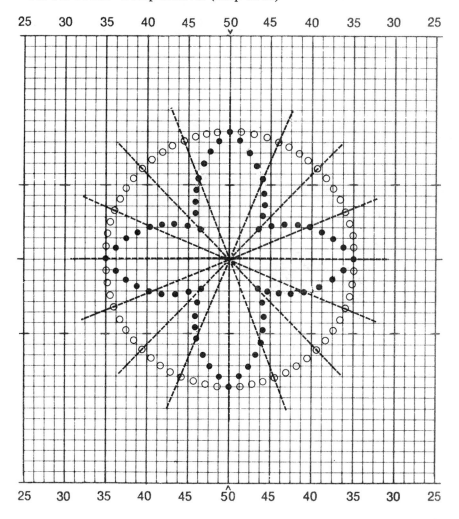

Example 3 illustrates the same flower petals using two circles of 64 players.

Example 3—(128 Players: 64 + 64)
Flower Petals—2-step interval (Step-twos)

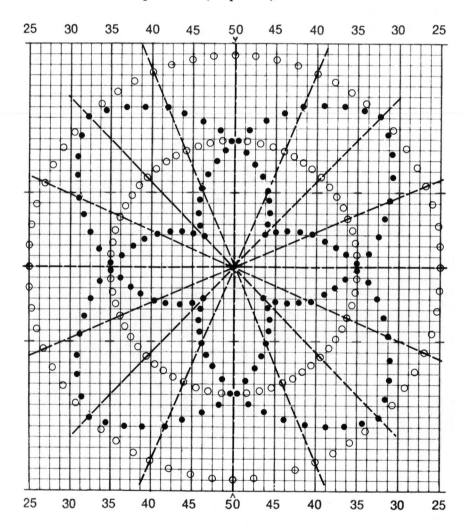

If you use circles of 48 players (which combine to circles of 96 players) your flower will have six petals rather than four. As we stated earlier, circles of 96 players are an ideal size for these types of drills.

Example 4—(96 Players)
Flower Petals—2-step interval (Step-twos)

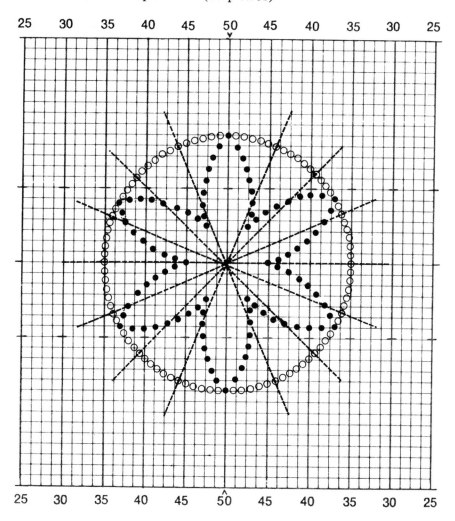

Example 5—(192 Players: 96 + 96)
Flower Petals—2-step interval (Step-twos)

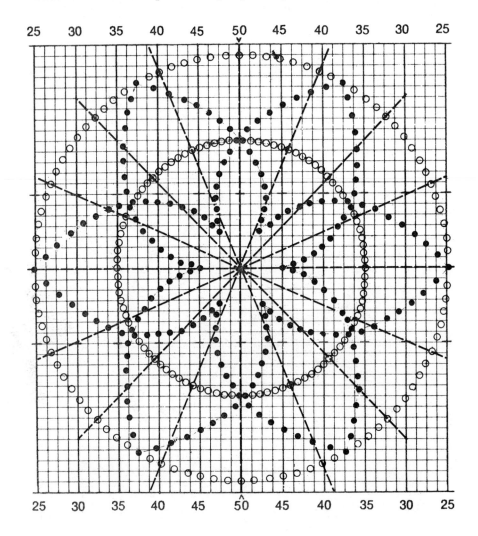

Another interesting variation is created by changing the position of your stationary players.

Example 6—(128 Players: 64 + 64)
Concentric Flowers—2-step interval (Step-twos)

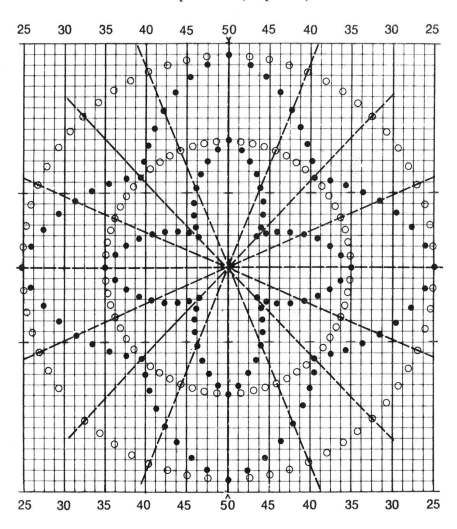

Spirals are another variation that can be very easily set up. Once again, while they can be performed with a single circle of 64 players, they are even more effective with the larger groups of players.

Example 7—(64 Players)
Spirals—2-step interval (Step-twos)

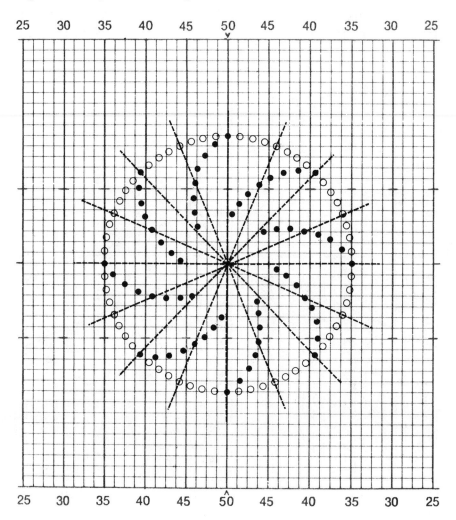

Example 8—(128 Players)
Spirals—2-step interval (Step-twos)

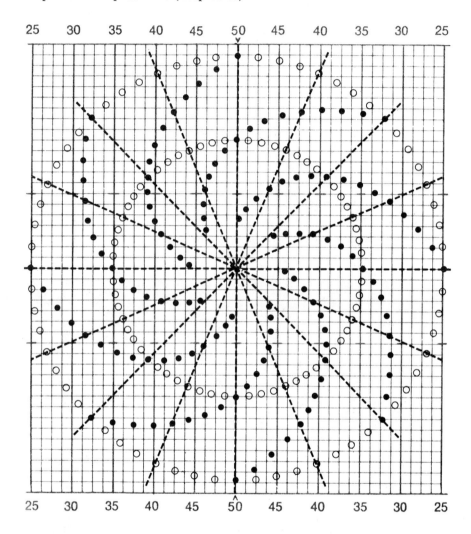

The number of ways that circles can be combined into interesting new patterns is again limited only by the teacher's imagination and creativity. Circles can go to boxes (squares); diamonds; stars; and to each other in numerous different ways which time and space will not allow us to demonstrate at this time.

Circles are fun for both the marchers and the audience. If you have never used them before, you will probably be very pleasantly surprised and pleased with the reaction you will receive from your audience the first time you present these or other variations.

The drills and devices that have been presented up to this point are designed to take the guess-work out of marching shows and their preparation. By working with consistent guidelines and fundamentals, drills can be prepared and taught much more quickly, more efficiently, more pleasantly, and more safely. This more scientific approach is of no less importance in the other areas of marching band performance, and we shall try to organize and clarify basic formations in the next chapter.

11
Multiple Option
Drill Techniques IV
Formations

Practically every band and teacher has, at some time, had the opportunity or been faced with the need to form a formation of some sort. Formations can be a very safe device if the teacher is aware of the basic rules and guidelines which make this part of the show virtually foolproof. If you have wondered how some bands are able to form such beautiful, uniform, nicely proportioned formations, letters, and designs, this chapter should provide you with some interesting information which will enable you to design them and produce them for your own band.

Formations

Traditionally there have been four basic techniques used to place players in their proper positions in formations:
1. Scatter System
2. Small Unit Drills (like 4-player squads)
3. Follow-the-Leader
4. Rank Leader Drills

1. Scatter System

   One of the early and most commonly used systems of forming letters or pictures on a football field was by identifying every position on the formation chart, having the players simply "break" from their previous positions and get to their new positions any way they were able. This obviously works; however, it suffers in visual appearance when compared with the more orderly methods which came later. It has two distinct disadvantages in that every individual has to memorize his exact position and his own route to it; and it takes longer to teach than any of the three systems described below. Too frequently, when scattering, a band will look like a confused lost group of individuals, rather than an orderly, well drilled marching unit that clearly knows where it is going.

2. Small Unit (or Squad) Drills

   For years these have been used most effectively by good drill bands and obviously are most practical when making formations that involve straight lines and distinct angles rather than curves; or, crooked lines such as those in an outline of the United States.

Establishing a uniform drill into school letters can be an effective device in a standardized pre-game show, or as a traditional ending for a half-time show. Many school initials lend themselves well to this sort of planning.

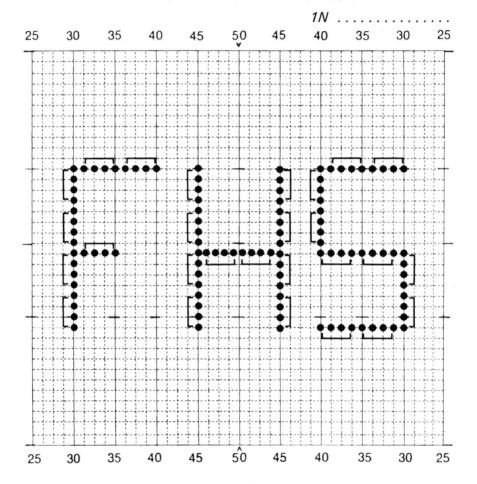

Another example of an effective formation that can be built using Drills by Squads is illustrated in example 2N on page 214. This simple formation provides a "Stairway to the Stars" for the presentation of a Homecoming Sweetheart or Queen. She and her escort can begin on the 25 yard line and walk to the center of the field where she can be presented on an elevated podium or platform.

Formations

The stairs illustrated use only 40 players. If more are available a second set of steps can descend to the 25 yard line on the reader's right, or an additional formation can be formed in the center, above the top step: a square, circle, star, or school initials can be attractive and lend themselves to this sort of presentation.

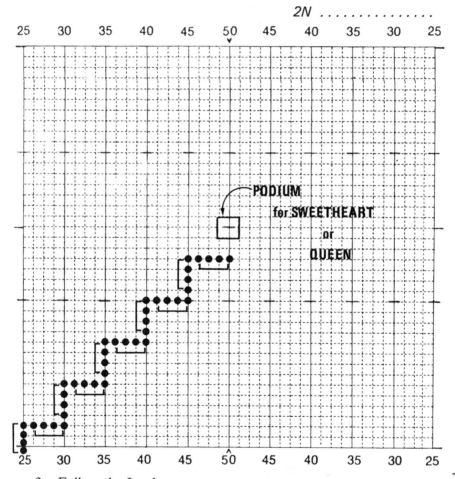

3. Follow-the-Leader

One of the most effective and safest means of forming an outline or letters is by establishing key "lead off" players. These are directed to their route along with the necessary number of persons needed for that portion of the formation following them single-file into their positions. This has a number of distinct and obvious advantages over the two systems described earlier: 1) The "leader" can concentrate on the route and everyone following can rely on the leader for direction, thus being able to concentrate on playing. 2) This is visually effective and, if properly set up, the audience can watch the outline being formed by a moving line. The effect is similar to watching a drawing take shape. 3) This is especially appropriate when forming "script" letters, or large, curved-line, continuous formations like maps, treble clef signs, etc.

In the example which is illustrated below, the band's starting position is double ranks of 16 players each. The "lead-off" man is A2 who is then followed by B2, A1, and B1; B3 then moves out following B1, and the rest of AB follows in numerical order. When A8 passes C4, C4 must be standing beside the 45 yard line, to lead off CD 1-4, who finish the formation. CD 5 through 8 wait for the next part of the formation.

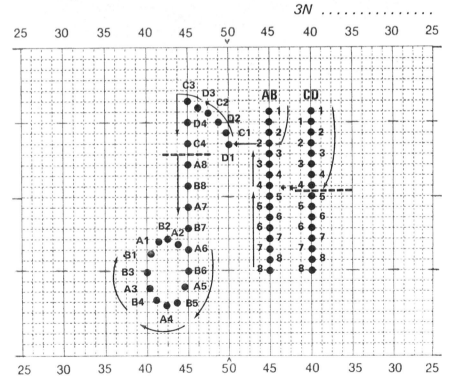

215

This photo shows the University of Texas Longhorn Band, Vincent R. DiNino, Director, in their famous script Texas formation. For many years the Texas band has made excellent use of follow-the-leader drills.

University of Texas Longhorn Band's "script" Texas

4. Rank Leader Drills

This system has the advantage of being able to make use of many of the best features of the other systems, and at the same time provide an opportunity for utilizing and encouraging student leadership. It has the unique feature of allowing the student to be a part of the actual creative process, rather than just being one person in a line of people necessary for the performançe of a pre-existing idea.

A. Freely Structured R.L. Drills

Rank leaders may be instructed to establish their routing with no limitation other than time or a set number of counts to restrict their ingenuity or creativity. They must be given charts showing their final stopping position in the formation. They can then be encouraged to create interesting patterns, designs, or drill sequences, and the result can be both fun and exciting.

B. Structured R.L. Drills

The Rank Leader Drills can be structured in a general way so that they fit more effectively into the style, or form, of an individual show. To achieve the "drawing" effect on maps, script, or curved designs, rank leaders can be instructed to move into position single-file, or by the follow-the-leader process described in #3. Or, to achieve a "drill" effect, they can be instructed to make all moves using 4-player squads and the appropriate Squad Drill devices.

C. Structured Routing

If it seems expeditious or necessary for some reason, the exact routing can be prescribed and the rank leaders then provide the leadership for its immediate and most effective execution. In this way they continue to develop leadership, be more involved, and actually function as student-assistant directors and links in an orderly "chain of command."

Formation Guidelines

There are a limited number of basic rules which, if followed consistently, enable us to set up formations relatively quickly, and at the same time guarantee a high level of visibility and uniformity.

1. Horizontal Interval

Players standing in a line parallel to the sidelines should be spaced at an interval of 1¼ yards, or two 22½ inch steps, apart. This places three people between the yard lines, with one standing on each line. It is the smallest number of players that connect visually to give the illusion of a continuous straight line when viewed from the sidelines. (See example 4N.)

2. Vertical Interval

Players standing on a yard line and facing downfield (toward either end zone) would stand with the *arch* of the foot on the yard line, centering the body over the line.

Players standing on a yard line and facing the sideline should "center" their bodies over the line, with the center of the line running between their feet (which are together). Normal spacing in a line parallel to or on a yard line is from two to four paces apart, with the most standard spacing being four paces (2½ yards).

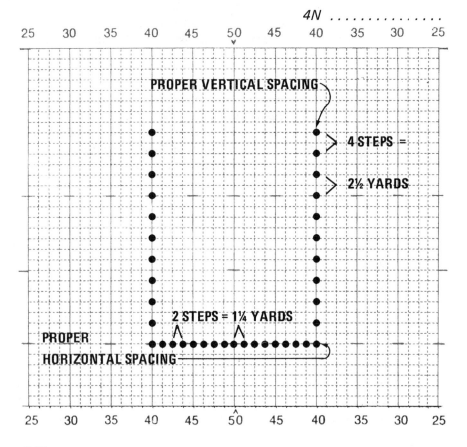

4N

*Vertical and horizontal spacing in a staging formation
by the University of Kansas Band.*

3. Charting a Curve

Charting a curved line can sometimes present difficulties.
Generally, if the line is basically horizontal there should
be three players between yard lines, keeping the same
basic interval as a horizontal line. If the curved line is
basically vertical, fewer people are needed for the eye to
connect them visually into a constant line. However, the
vertical spacing ideally should never exceed a distance
of 2½ yards.

219

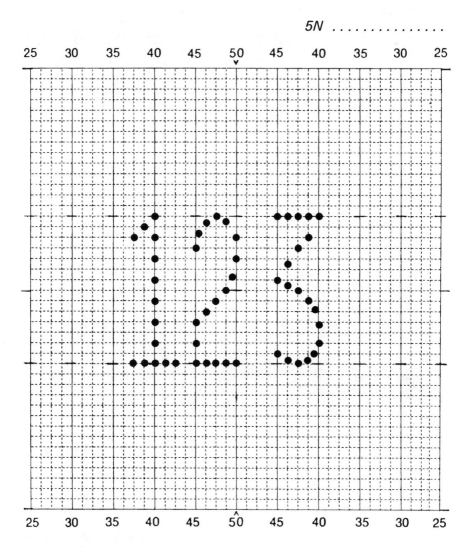

4. Extra People

Since it is not uncommon for a formation to require slightly fewer people than are available, a question that frequently arises is "What do I do with the extra people?" There are several obvious solutions to the above problem, one of which is simply to march the extras off to the sideline farthest from the main audience. A better solution, however, is to "hide" these extras in the vertical lines. While extra people in a horizontal line are very obvious and undesirable, extras in the vertical lines are very easily concealed from a sideline bleacher. (If there is an end zone television camera, then there is another problem, and it will be desirable to keep vertical lines balanced as carefully as the horizontals.) Generally speaking, as a spectator looks down two parallel vertical lines, as in the sides of an "H," there is little or no difference in the appearance of a side using 8 players or one using 9. Example 6N uses 70 men. It would have been just as easy to use 68 by dropping one player from the "H" and one from the "P."

6N . . . .

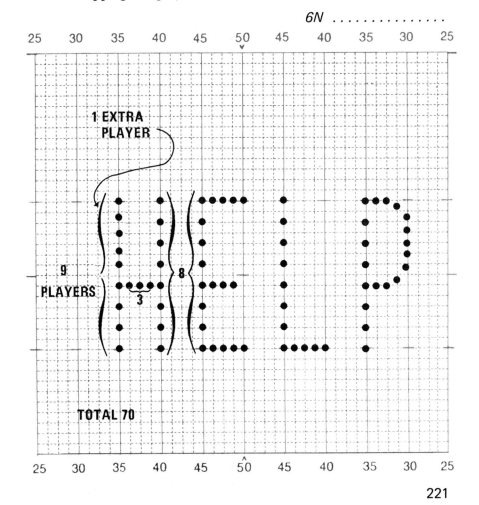

Formations

If there is quite a large number of people to be placed, it is sometimes effective to use them in a "staging" position or to help frame the formation. At times it is appropriate to place all, or most of an entire section to the front to be featured, taking them out of the formation as shown in example 7N. They can march to their position at the same time that the rest of the band moves into the formation.

7N ....

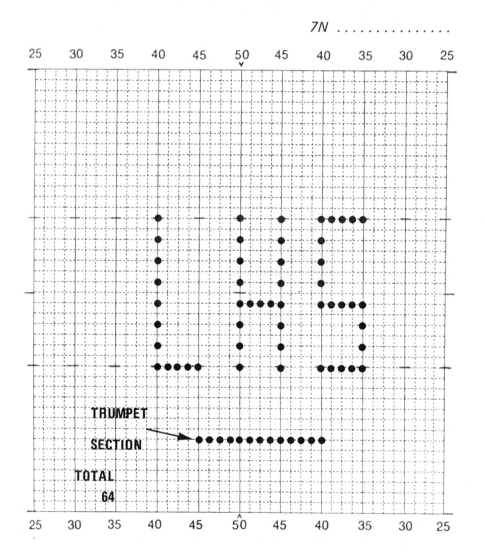

TRUMPET SECTION TOTAL 64

222

*Formation illustrating block letters, charted curves,
angles, and hidden extra people.*

5. Block Letters

Excellent and almost foolproof letters can be formed using
the standard formation spacing (2 steps apart from left to
right and 4 steps apart from front to rear as viewed from the
sideline). This again places three players between the yard
lines with one player on each line, so letters are five yards
wide; and eight players in the vertical lines, placing one on
each hash mark. An eight-man rank can therefore become the
vertical side of a letter very easily. Using the hash marks for
the top and bottom, uniform block letters of excellent propor-
tion and perspective can be formed (see examples 6N and 7N).

6. Perspective

One factor that must be kept constantly in mind when drawing and charting formations is the perspective of a formation as viewed from a bleacher on one side. For example, a perfect circle executed on the field becomes almost egg-shaped when viewed from the side. The lower the stands are, the flatter the circle will look.

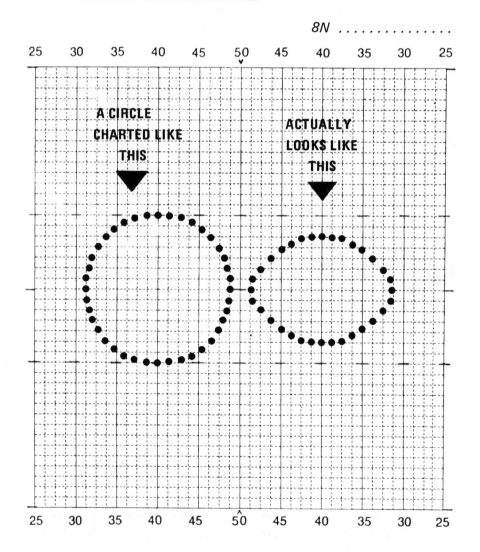

To properly chart formations so they are viewed as we expect them to be, it is normally necessary to make all figures or designs much taller than they would be on a flat drawing. A normal stick figure will become a short, squat figure. To produce a normal stick figure, it is necessary to chart one that is quite tall and elongated.

7. Instrument Placement

If the band is playing specifically to one stand of persons (as compared with trying to disperse sound evenly throughout a large bowl type stadium), group the instruments that you wish to be heard most prominently as close to the sidelines as possible. For example, if a flute and woodwind number is being featured, the flutes and woodwinds should be the players nearest the audience. For a number featuring the percussion, they should be out in front. The percussion section should always be placed together as a section, and normally, it should be as near the center of the formation as possible. If for some reason the percussion section has to be divided, all percussionists must listen extremely carefully. Should precision and ensemble problems occur, they must play more softly so they can hear the band. Sometimes it may become necessary to have those players who are the greatest distance from the main portion of the section stop playing entirely and simply "fake it," pretending to play, but making no sound.

When grouping instruments in a formation in order to obtain the maximum sound—the most (but best quality) sound possible—a general formula may be followed: Percussion are grouped as a section and placed in the center of the band (if the percussion are too heavy, they can be moved farther back); trumpets are placed in the front and center, followed by trombones and baritones; horns and saxes are next, followed by clarinets and flutes. Basses may be placed on the outside of the formation behind the trombones and baritones, or for a better visual effect they might be placed at the back (top) of the formation.

This basic formula has proved to be particularly effective for getting more and better sound picked up by the mikes used for network telecasts.

225

8. "Dressing" a Line

When the formation calls for a straight line which is not on a yard line, all players in the line should move into it so that they can "dress" the line (check alignment) looking from side to side, rather than from the front to the back. After "dressing the line" they should then turn to face the sideline. The turn to the sideline may be marked either at a specific point in the music, or it can be accomplished as a "ripple turn," as each bandsman turns immediately after the one beside him. If a "ripple" turn is used, the "ripple" should begin at the end of the line on that side the formation will face so that each turning bandsman can easily check his alignment immediately after turning. You can't "dress" to a line which has formed behind you. You need to be behind (or beside) someone for best alignment.

9. Heels and Toes

When standing motionless in any formation, keep *heels and toes* together. This avoids a lack of uniformity which is so noticeable on televised marching performances, when so many feet are pointing out at slightly different angles. It provides a white (or a black) block of color at the feet of each bandsman, rather than uneven "Vs" which are created by separated feet of differing lengths.

10. Moving Formations

When moving a formation downfield, always use a uniform 22½ inch (8 to 5) step unless there is a need for a step of different size, in which case the desired step size should be specified.

11. Formation Examples

The following formations have been used by various well-known marching bands, and are based on the principles and concepts which have been discussed.

The University of Florida Gator Band forms outline of the state in Miami's Orange Bowl. This formation was formed with rank leaders and "follow-the-leader" techniques.

Formations

The University of Florida Gator Band in a simple block band drill and staging formation.

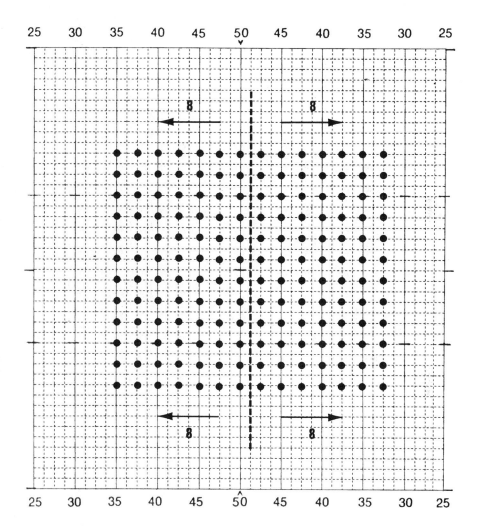

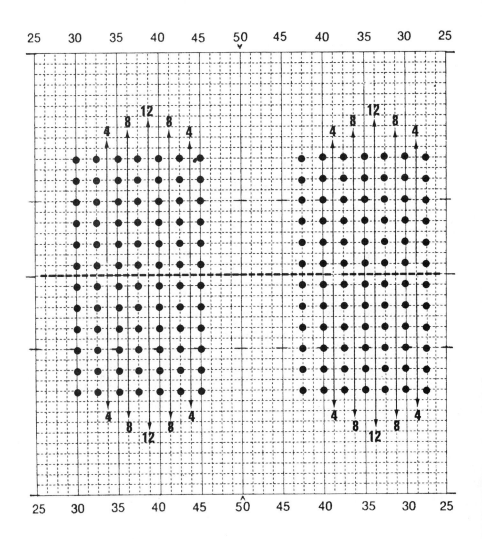

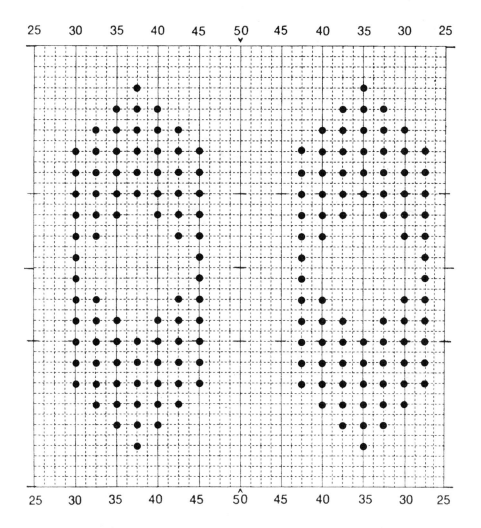

The University of Kansas Band in a different concert formation.

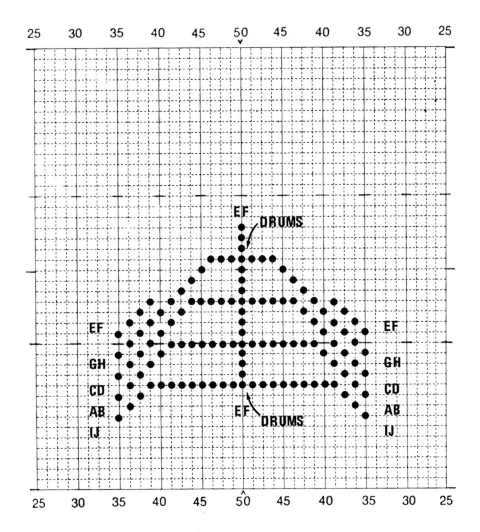

Riverboat—The Robert E. Lee

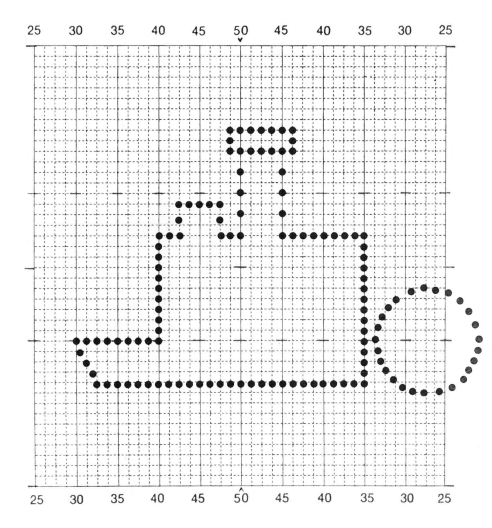

The Wabash Cannonball

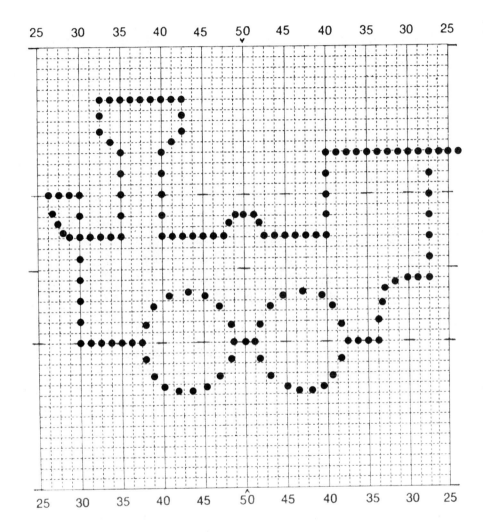

25 30 35 40 45 50 45 40 35 30 25

25 30 35 40 45 50 45 40 35 30 25

Traditional pre-game formation by the University of Kansas Band.

Up until now, we have discussed some of the more important concepts and principles which are necessary for a band to function successfully on a football field; we have discussed the fundamentals and devices necessary to perform most types of drills, and you have seen many examples of drills and formations with suggestions as to how they can be taught. There still remain many questions, however, regarding musical factors, instrument placement, and the preparation of a script. These details will be discussed in the chapter that follows.

12
Special Problems
of the Marching Band

Instrument Placement; Playing; Preparing a Script

There are basic guidelines which will be helpful in determining where personnel should be placed, yet there is no single rule or formula that can satisfy the needs of, or solve the problems for every band in every situation.

The location of various sections of the band will vary depending on the type of music performed, the kind of sound desired, and the nature of the formation in which the band is standing or marching. Improper or illogical placement of personnel in a marching formation can cause severe balance problems both musically and visually.

Instrument Placement

There are many factors in addition to just marching and playing that contribute to producing an impressive and totally successful marching band. Among these are the format of the show itself; the placement of the instruments in a formation or on the field; the image that is created by the announcer and announcements; and the playing quality—both of what is played and how it is played. This chapter attempts to deal with these various problems, which, when handled properly, frequently make the difference between an outstanding image and one that is merely good.

It is a good general rule that, whenever possible, instruments of the same type should be grouped together. This makes it easier for the sections to play together while also providing a more attractive visual picture. A long row of trumpets or horns lined up uniformly simply looks better than a line of trumpets with a flute and a clarinet or two mixed in, and the same idea holds true in almost every section.

Another good generalization is that percussion should be grouped as closely together as possible and, unless they are being featured as a solo or soli section, they should be in the middle of the band slightly toward the rear of a formation. However, a strong percussion section can create a "wall of sound" making it difficult to hear instruments placed immediately behind them. Also, players standing near, or behind the percussion may have difficulty hearing sections that are located on the opposite side of the band.

Because of their great visibility, tubas or sousaphones usually look best along the sides or at the back of a formation (either stationary or moving). Since they are so large, they could create visual problems for students located behind them who are attempting to see a conductor or a drum major.

When preparing a formation for a performance to be televised, it is desirable to limit the width of the formation so that the band is not spread the length of the field. If players are grouped toward the center, the chances of getting both good video and good audio pickup are greatly improved. Camera and microphone are both limited when it comes to covering an entire field.

Block Band

A 64 piece block band might be set up like this:

Tubas can be on the corners of the back row (H1 and H8), or on the corners of the front (low brass) rows (A1 and A8).

This basic set-up is similar to the traditional placement of instruments in military bands. It looks good to have a whole row of trombones, or six trombones (or four if you march six across) flanked by two tubas. It allows plenty of "slide" room for the trombones, and stacks your brass power up front for greater impact. This is most ideal for "power" playing pop tunes, show tunes, and special arrangements. However, it is also particularly effective with traditional

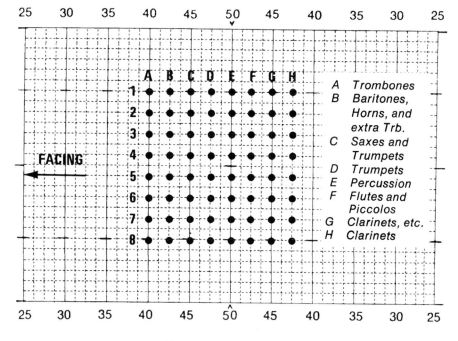

| 25 | 30 | 35 | 40 | 45 | 50 | 45 | 40 | 35 | 30 | 25 |

A Trombones
B Baritones,
  Horns, and
  extra Trb.
C Saxes and
  Trumpets
D Trumpets
E Percussion
F Flutes and
  Piccolos
G Clarinets, etc.
H Clarinets

FACING

64- piece Block Band set-up.

marches with low brass melody (like the trio of National Emblem, or the first half of March Grandioso).

D Rank and C Rank may be switched so the saxes are behind the trumpets. This will result in more brilliance and predominant trumpet (or cornet) sound, but it will also weaken the audibility of the inner voices. Saxophones tend to be good reinforcers of horn and baritone voices and while not necessarily distinguishable as a section outside, they do make valuable contributions to the total sound—especially in depth, fullness, and color. The relative strength of sections will vary from one year to another. If you have particularly strong trombones and comparatively weaker trumpets, experiment with the trumpets in front of the trombones. Then you will have in the front of your band your strongest melody voice followed by your strongest countermelody voice. Don't ever hesitate to change the placement of your personnel if you can strengthen your performance by doing so. Also, by altering the placement of your personnel, you can frequently solve or avoid personality conflicts between students, distribute leadership more effectively, and adjust for better balance and blend as well as power.

The following is another basic block band set-up that is especially useful with the younger or less mature band. This set-up more closely follows the traditional concert band seating arrangement with the weaker voices in the front and the stronger voices behind them. It is particularly useful for producing a more "symphonic" sound outside.

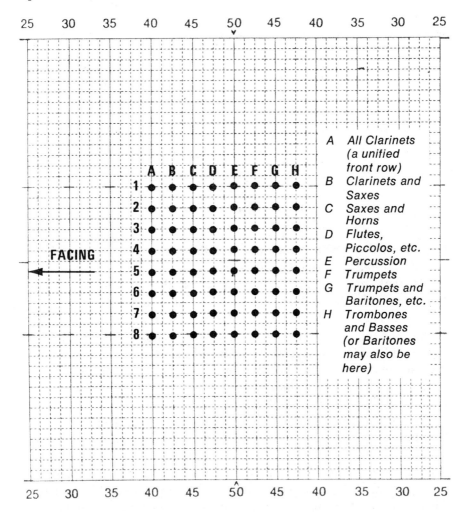

A	All Clarinets (a unified front row)
B	Clarinets and Saxes
C	Saxes and Horns
D	Flutes, Piccolos, etc.
E	Percussion
F	Trumpets
G	Trumpets and Baritones, etc.
H	Trombones and Basses (or Baritones may also be here)

Formations

Instrument placement in picture or letter outlines, in stationary or moving formations closely follows the order of the block band examples. For more power, stack the brass toward the front and center; for more "symphonic" balance and woodwind color, bring the woodwinds forward.

For maximum power in a picture formation (like a map, box, or letters) try to stack your brass up front something like this:

Clarinets - - - - Flutes - - - - Clarinets

Saxes   Percussion   Saxes

Tuba   Tuba

Horns-Baritones   Horns-Baritones

Trombones - - - - - - - Trumpets - - - - - - - Trombones

sideline _____(front)

or,

Clarinets - - - - Flutes - - - - Clarinets

Clarinets   Percussion   Clarinets

Tuba   Saxes   Saxes   Tuba

Horns-Baritones   Horns-Baritones

Trombones - - - - - - - Trumpets - - - - - - - Trombones

sideline _____ (front)

243

Entry Formation

For more brilliance in your entry fanfare, try bringing the trumpets to the very front and center like this (using rank numbers from the first block illustration in this unit):

(F Rank—flutes)
X X X X X X X X

(G1-4 cl)   (H Rank—clarinets)   (G5-8 cl)
X X X X X X X X X X X X X X X X

(E Rank—percussion)
X X X X (X X X X X X X X) X X X X

(B1-4 hns)   (C Rank—trpts & sax)   (B5-8 bar)
X X X X X X X X X X X X X X X X

(A1-4 trb)   (D Rank—trumpets)   (A5-8 trb)
X X X X X X X X X X X X X X X X

Drum Major

or, try it with the flutes beside the percussion:

(F1-4 fl)   (E Rank—percussion)   (F5-8 fl)
X X X X X X X X X X X X X X X X

and, place the sousaphones on the outsides of the first, or the first two rows (A1 and A8, or A1, B1, and A8, B8).

Playing

Performers should improve as players throughout the football season. The brass especially can use this experience to develop better breath support, endurance, and general strength. Students should not be permitted to overblow and get resultant bad sounds to succeed in marching band, nor should they be allowed to play with bad embouchures and improper hand positions anymore than they should in a concert situation. Two factors in marching technique directly affect playing ability while marching: 1) The six steps to five yards, or corps style 8 to 5, a "stride step," a smooth gait very conducive to better playing. When done correctly, the player simply strides smoothly, striking the ground with his heels first. There is very little motion above the waist, except for a slight natural "swagger." 2) When marching eight steps to five yards with a high knee lift, there need be almost no motion above the waist if this is properly executed. But this cannot be done flat-footed. The player must march "on his toes!" When the foot leaves the ground, "peel" it off the ground from the heel forward, the toe leaving the ground last. Lift the leg from the hip, keeping the toe pointed toward the ground. When the foot returns to the ground, the toe strikes first, and the entire foot functions as a "shock absorber" or spring, eliminating almost all "bounce." As in the six to five stride, the only noticeable movement above the waist should be a smooth swagger from left to right. Students must be *shown* and taught how to do this correctly.

The MUSIC MUST COME FIRST. We must keep in mind that a marching band has two basic functions: to march well, and to *play* well. The choice of music for the marching band is of paramount importance: 1) It must be matched to the technical ability of each individual group; 2) it must be appropriate to the drill or formation with which it is intended to be presented; and 3) it must be satisfying (or entertaining) to everyone involved (the director, students, and audience). If the director and his students are "turned off" by a corny arrangement, the chances are very good that the audience will be "turned off" by it too.

One must ask the question whether teachers stop to realize that their musical tastes and judgment are evaluated by many thousands of people every fall, just as their musical taste is evaluated by concert goers in the concert hall. Whether one likes it or not, his marching band *does* reflect his personal tastes and judgment. If more directors were fully aware of this, they would probably be much more careful in their selection of music for their marching band.

The marching band at its best is a very basic form of choreography. It is motion set to music on a very large scale for a very large audience. Historically, the successful choreography of great ballets has generally been linked to great music. A great dance set to mediocre music has little chance for lasting success. Nor does a mediocre dance to great music have any greater future. A strong parallel to this can be drawn in our marching performances. It is no less important for us to be as discriminating and careful in selecting good and appropriate music for such performances.

Preparing a Script

An announcer with a pleasing voice and good timing can be an asset to any fine band, while an announcer with an unexciting voice, or one who is not properly prepared will be a detriment. Many school bands have this problem and it usually is a result of one of two factors; or in some cases, both factors.

The Announcer

Far too many teachers fail to take advantage of the good public relations that can be enjoyed through utilizing a popular local businessman or administrator who has public speaking experience. This is a great way to get community people more involved in your program. Another source for good announcers is frequently available through your speech and drama teachers. This is excellent practical training for a student interested in speech, announcing, or dramatics; and most speech teachers appreciate having the opportunity to select their outstanding students for this experience. Regardless of who is selected to be the announcer, it should be understood that he will attend enough rehearsals prior to the performance that both he and the band are secure in their timing.

The Script

Many half-time show announcers apparently never have a chance to do a professional job of announcing because they are not given a good, well-prepared script. This is as much a part of the director's responsibility as the rest of the preparation of the show! We spend thousands of dollars on beautiful uniforms and hours of work preparing music and drills, yet some of us apparently are not willing to spend a few more minutes in order to present a better, more professional image in this important area. An outstanding announcer with a good script is an important factor in creating a favorable atmosphere for a band performance.

A script should be basically simple, easy to read and understand. It must contain enough information so that a non-musician can follow the action on the field, and contain all necessary instructions to the announcer, as well as the announcements he should make. It should also be interesting and informative to the audience.

If a performance is to be televised, it is suggested that the script contain a diagram of the important formations on the field with the cumulative timing running from the beginning of the show to the end. Also included should be the script and instructions, individual timing of each number, the titles and composer and/or arranger of each song performed, and their publisher, when possible.

Statements which are to be read by the announcer should be in capital letters, and should be double spaced.

Network announcers also appreciate background information about the band, its personnel, and the institution it represents. They particularly appreciate information about anything, or anyone, that is a little unusual or out of the ordinary. It is, therefore, a good idea to prepare a page of general information which the announcer can use at his own discretion. Professional announcers also point out that the scripts which are attractive and easy to read naturally get better attention from those in the press box than do scripts which are carelessly prepared.

(Sample Script—Pre-game)

Pre-Game Show of
The University of Kansas Marching Jayhawks

The Oklahoma Game—November 13

Formation	Time	Script	Music
		"LADIES AND GENTLEMEN, YOUR ATTENTION IS DIRECTED TO THE NORTH END OF THE STADIUM FOR THE ENTRANCE OF THE UNIVERSITY OF KANSAS JAYHAWK BAND."	(:25)

Formation	*Time*	*Script*	*Music*

(Band runs out to company fronts, and steps off immediately with the music, "Home on the Range." After four more loud measures, announcer says:)

:25 — "KU'S FAMOUS MARCHING JAYHAWKS PARADE THE FIELD TO A NEW ARRANGEMENT OF THE STATE SONG OF KANSAS. — "Home on the Range" arr. Robert Foster. (:55)

(Band continues marching and playing. After four more loud measures, announcer says:)

"UNDER DIRECTOR OF BANDS ROBERT FOSTER, ASSISTED BY GEORGE BOBERG AND DAVID BUSHOUSE, THE BAND IS LED ON THE FIELD BY DRUM MAJORS DAVID KOENIG AND BILL LAASER."

(Band reaches mid-field and changes direction, and moves into KU formation. Music ends, and band segues into "Fighting Jayhawk." After band begins to move, announcer says:)

1:20 — "MOVING TO THE STRAINS OF THE MARCH, 'FIGHTING JAYHAWK,' THE BAND MOVES TO MID-FIELD, AND FORMS CIRCLES SYMBOLIC OF THE CLOSED SUNFLOWER." — "Fighting Jayhawk" arr. William Davis (1:10)

(After "fight strain," band stands fast until end of "Fighting Jayhawk," then starts quickly playing "Sunflower Song." As movement becomes apparent, announcer says:)

Formation	Time	Script	Music
	2:30	"AS THE BAND PLAYS 'SUN-FLOWER SONG,' THE KANSAS SUNFLOWER BLOOMS." (Music continues, and band performs circle drill. Near the end of circle drill Pom-Pon Girls enter. As they enter, announcer says:)	"Sunflower Song" arr. David Bushouse (1:00)
		"AND NOW WE FEATURE THE 197. . . POM-PON GIRLS: DEBBIE KAMITSUKA, MARCIA ROBERT-SON, CHERYL WILLIAMS, SUE TAGG, ROSILAND FELLS, PEGGY SCOTT, AND CO-CAPTAINS, JANE PHELPS AND GLORIA JAHN."	
	3:30	(Music ends, Pom-Pon Girls exit, and band swings into straight lines, and exits playing. After band begins playing, announcer says:)	"I'm A Jayhawk" arr. James Barnes (:30)
		"THERE THEY GO LADIES AND GENTLEMEN: THE UNIVERSITY OF KANSAS MARCHING JAY-HAWKS. DIRECTOR OF BANDS IS ROBERT E. FOSTER. ASSISTANT DIRECTORS ARE GEORGE BOBERG AND DAVID BUSHOUSE. MUSICAL ARRANGER IS JAMES BARNES."	

Total: 4:00

(Sample Script—Half-time)

Half-time Show of
The University of Kansas Marching Jayhawks

The Oklahoma Game—November 13

Formation	Time	Script	Music
		(Trumpets and Drums enter center of field silently. Drum Major calls band to attention, and starts the drums and trumpets playing the cavalry charge, and band starts to enter with a slow step. After the second "Charge" drums break into fast cadence, and everyone charges onto the field fast. As fast tempo starts, announcer says:)	"Charge" (:35)
		"LADIES AND GENTLEMEN: THE UNIVERSITY OF KANSAS MARCHING JAYHAWKS!"	
	:35	(Band stops and moves into fanfare position and plays fanfare. Immediately after fanfare, band steps off playing "Scarborough Fair." As soon as music and motion are apparent, announcer says:)	"New Blue Fanfare" by Robert Foster (:15)
	:45	"THE KU BAND SALUTES OKLAHOMA'S RETURNING ALUMNI WITH THE THEME MUSIC FROM THE MOVIE, 'THE GRADUATE': 'SCARBOROUGH FAIR'." ("Scarborough Fair" ends, and band segues into "California Soul." After intro, announcer says:)	"Scarborough Fair" (folk-rock march) arr. Robert Foster (:40)

250

Formation	*Time*	*Script*	*Music*
	:55	"CONTINUING WITH MUSIC FROM ANOTHER GREAT STATE, THE BAND PLAYS 'CALIFORNIA SOUL,' AS THE BAND PERFORMS AN INTRI-CATE 'CIRCLE DRILL'." (Band finishes "California Soul," and segues into "The Dude." As music begins, say:)	"California Soul" arr. John Edmondson (1:00)
	1:55	"AND MORE CIRCLES ARE COMING, AS THE BAND CONTINUES ITS DRILL WITH A NEW ROCK MARCH CALLED 'THE DUDE'." (Band finishes in concentric circles; kneels and rises; and segues into "Get It." As soon as music starts, announcer says:)	"The Dude" by Robert Foster (1:40)
	3:35	WE PRESENT A SPECIAL NUMBER FEATURING KU'S FAMOUS POM-PON GIRLS: A NUMBER CALLED: 'GET IT'."	"Get It" arr. James Barnes (1:45)
	5:20	(Band finishes and immediately segues into "Stand Up and Cheer," and forms a large K. As soon as motion is apparent, say:) "WITH THE MUSIC 'STAND UP AND CHEER,' THE BAND FORMS A GIANT 'K,' IN A FINAL KU SALUTE."	"Stand Up Cheer" arr. James Barnes (:24)
		(Music stops with band in K, and band immediately breaks into "I'm A Jayhawk," changing the K into K A N S A S. Kansas formation remains through the	"I'm A Jayhawk" arr. James Barnes (:50)

251

Formation	Time	Script	Music
		"stop-time" music, and band turns and exits on the last half of the second time through the music. As the band starts moving off the field, say:)	
	5:44	"THERE THEY GO LADIES AND GENTLEMEN, THE UNIVER-SITY OF KANSAS MARCHING JAYHAWKS. DIRECTOR OF BANDS IS ROBERT E. FOSTER. ASSISTANT DIRECTORS ARE GEORGE BOBERG AND DAVID BUSHOUSE. MUSICAL ARRANGER IS JAMES BARNES. YOUR ANNOUNCER HAS BEEN DON SCHEID."	
	Total: 6:34		

(Sample "fact sheet" of additional information)

Facts About the KU Band

***The University of Kansas Marching Jayhawks includes 240 men and women musicians who represent all of the colleges within the University.

***The Band Department is in the School of Fine Arts, James Moeser, Dean, and includes three concert bands, two basketball bands, three jazz ensembles, and pep band in addition to the Marching Band.

***The KU Marching Band is joined at the games by the International Cheerleading Foundation's nationally ranked pep groups—the KU Yell Leaders and the KU Pom-Pon Girls.

Personnel

ROBERT E. FOSTER, Director of Bands, came to the Lawrence campus from the University of Florida, where he was Associate

Director of Bands. He has had extensive experience with marching bands at all educational levels, and is the composer/arranger of two new series of publications of marching band music. This December, for the third consecutive year, Mr. Foster will be musical director for the Gator Bowl in Jacksonville, Florida.

GEORGE BOBERG, Assistant Director of Bands and professor of percussion, was a professional percussionist in New York prior to coming to Kansas. He performed with some of the nation's leading percussion ensembles.

DAVID BUSHOUSE, Assistant Director, came to the University of Kansas from Morehead State University in Kentucky, where he was assistant band director and professor of french horn. He is in his third year at KU.

JAMES BARNES, Musical Arranger for the band is from Hobart, Oklahoma. A graduate of the University of Kansas, his arrangements have been widely played by high school and university bands throughout the nation.

Student Personnel

Head Drum Major, DAVID KOENIG, is a senior from St. Louis, Missouri, majoring in Business Administration.

Assistant Drum Major is BILL LAASER, a sophomore from Kansas City, majoring in Mathematics.

Band President, GARY McCARTY, is a percussionist majoring in Music. He is from Jacksonville, Illinois.

Librarian . . . . David Tallent, from Aurora, Colo.
Librarian . . . . Bruse Penner, from Topeka, Ks.
Equipment Manager . . . . Greg Clemons, from Ft. Scott, Ks.

Thoughtful placement of personnel, an able announcer, good music and fine playing, all combined with effective drills, precise formations, and good execution of consistent fundamentals are all important factors in attaining excellence with a marching band.

253

Preparing an exciting marching band performance which utilizes all these factors, together with good pacing and variety, is a challenge of the first order. In the next and final chapter we shall prepare a complete show for a 64 piece band utilizing the basic concepts and principles which have been presented and discussed.

Preparing Your Own Complete Show
(for 64 piece band)

This basic sample show will consist of the following:
1. A field entrance
2. Fanfare position and fanfare
3. Downfield march (or drill)
4. Precision drill routine
5. Musical feature from concert formation
   (Optional—add any other formation that may be desired with appropriate music at this point. Feature twirlers, flags, or other auxiliary units if desired.)
6. School salute formation
7. Exit

Show planning can begin with any facet of your show. We will take these items in the order that they occur during actual performance.

Field Entrance, Fanfare Position, and Fanfare

First we will select a fanfare position. Then we must establish a way for the band to get from the sideline, or behind the end zone, to that position.

A very simple, yet effective fanfare position is achieved by moving from the block band to a two-step interval as in Drills by Squads. Start with the front of the block (A Rank) on the 15 yard line (example A), and have even numbered ranks (B, D, F, H) FM4— moving to the right of the person in front of them (example B).

Example A   *Example B*

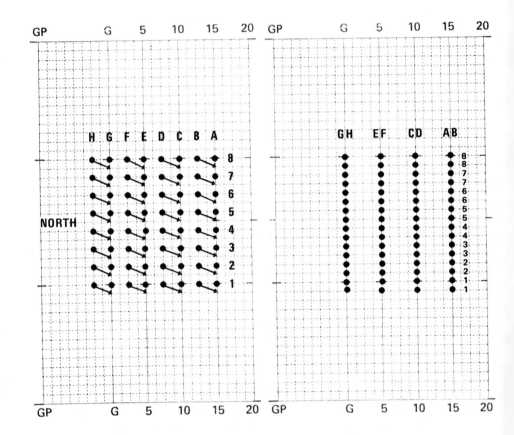

Next, determine how you wish to get to this position. Four options (starting from a position of attention and moving to a drum cadence) are:
1. All enter single file from one sideline (example C).

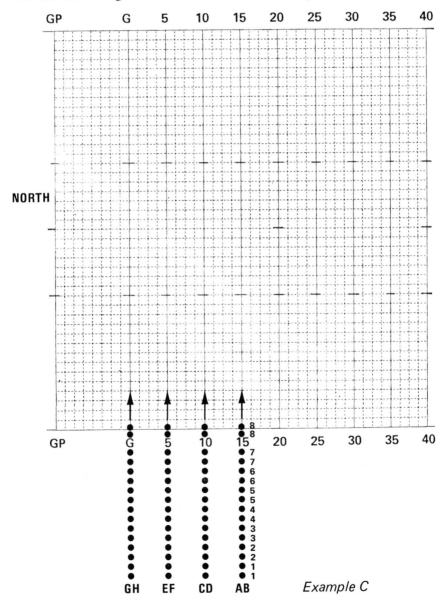

Example C

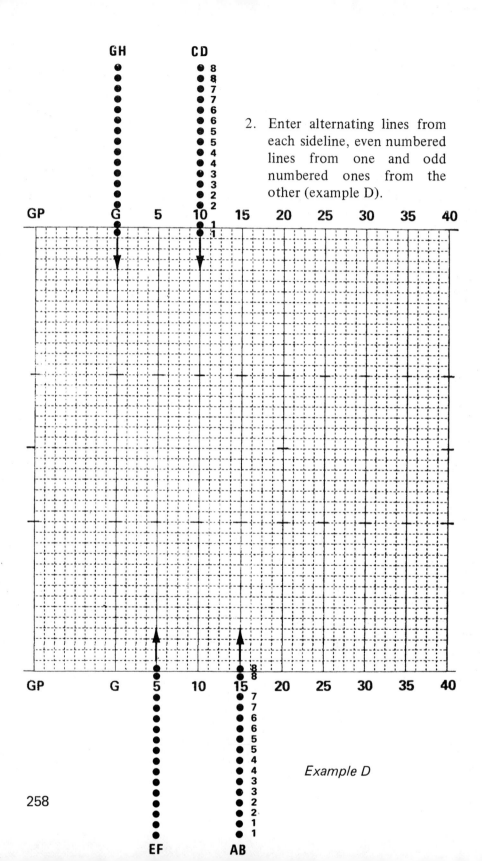

2. Enter alternating lines from each sideline, even numbered lines from one and odd numbered ones from the other (example D).

Example D

258

3. Enter all 1-4s from West sideline (pressbox side), and 5-8s from the opposite (East) side (example E).

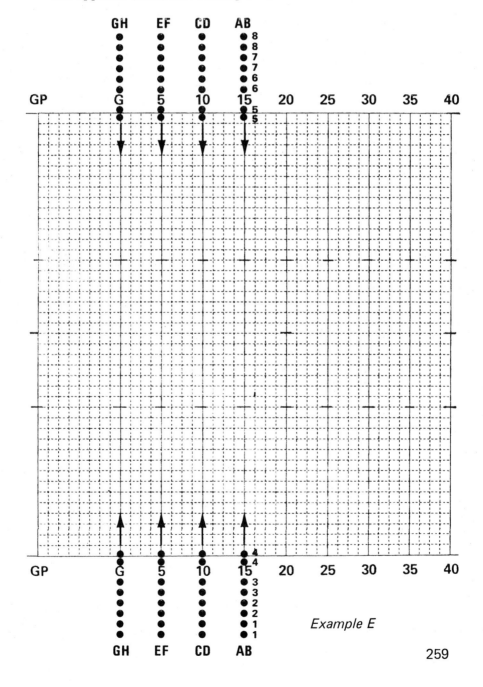

Example E

4. A more sophisticated entrance can be achieved by having the band stand in fanfare position (example B), About Face so they face North end zone, and all 1-4s do Left by Squads 8 (L/S8), and 5-8s do Right by Squads 8 (R/S 8) (example F) to position shown in example G.

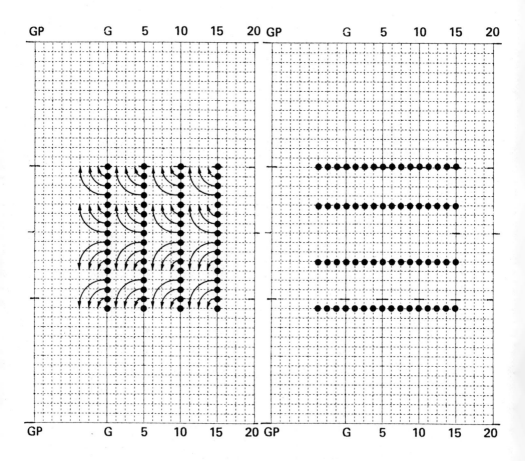

Example F   Example G

Then have the four new lines exit single file to the North, stopping in single file with the front person on the Goal Post line (example H).

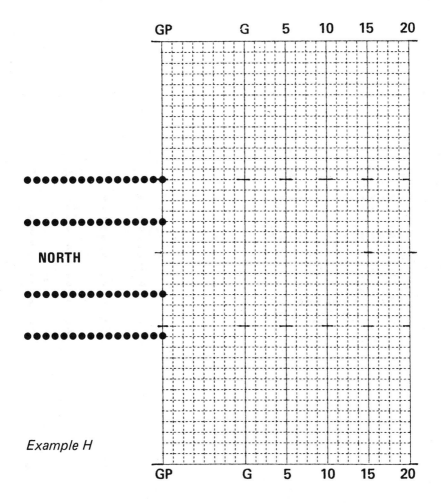

Example H

Have the lines face South and enter with a drum cadence, stopping in place (example G) with a Halt Cadence.

1-4s Left Flank, and R/S 8, H & C; and 5-8s Right Flank (RF), L/S 8, H & C (Hit and Close), stopping in the desired fanfare position (example I).

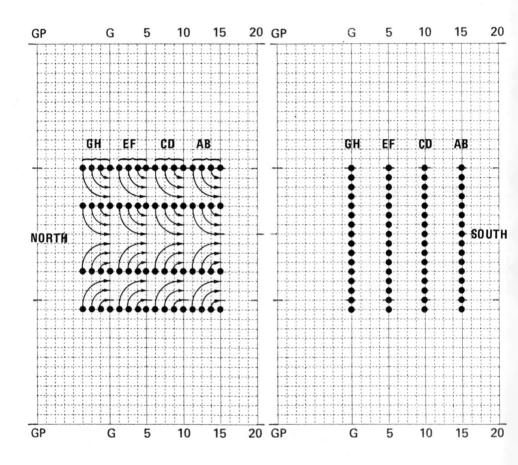

Example I

The next command must be a Raise Instruments, or it may be automatic on the next two counts after H & C, like: Hit and Close; Raise Instruments!

counts:	1	2	3	4	1
				(prepare)	(up!)
verbally say:	"Hit and Close!			and	UP!

The Fanfare is played in this position, standing at Attention.

Downfield March

At the conclusion of the fanfare, instruments remain up, and band is ready to begin Downfield March.

Select music that is solidly scored and do not hesitate to alter the music with cuts or repeats if it will help meet your needs. One chorus or strain of many standard songs or marches will be perfect to move the band 40 yards (8 sets of 8 counts—64 steps).

Now, from our Fanfare Position we have the option of returning to a block immediately or remaining in close interval fronts (lines). We shall return to the block in 4 steps by having the odd numbered ranks (A, C, E, etc.) FM (Forward March), and even numbered ranks (B, D, F, etc.) sidestep to the left 4. See illustration:

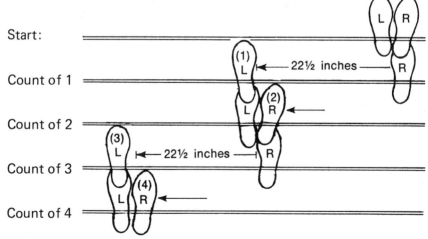

The Downfield March, or Drill may be charted, or written down like this:

Preparing Your Own Complete Show

Music: *Broadway Salute* (begin at Letter A)

Instructions:

A, C, E, G: FM 64; MT 4; H & C.

B, D, F, H: Side Step 4 to the Left; FM 60; MT 4; H & C.

Sample Solo Cornet part:

Broadway Salute

Precision Drill Routine

Block Band is now located with A Rank on the South 45 yard line. Since one of the most basic drills is the split Block Band Drill, we will begin with that type of drill, changing later to a Sliding

Geometrics Drill. Select music with some crowd appeal. We will use the Jazz-Rock selection: *Shoutin' Soul.*

Play the introduction standing fast, and begin marching at letter A; then, in order to provide maximum security of both playing and marching, we will set up the drill so that generally one half of the band will mark time in place, playing, while the other half moves and plays. (Music on page 275).

Music: *Shoutin' Soul* (see page 275).
Play introduction standing in place; step off marching at letter A.

Letter A
1. A-D: FM 8
    E-H: MT 8

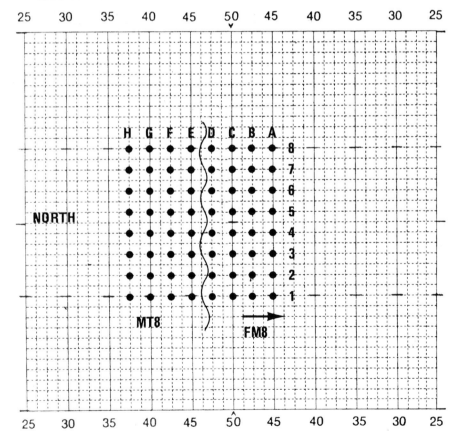

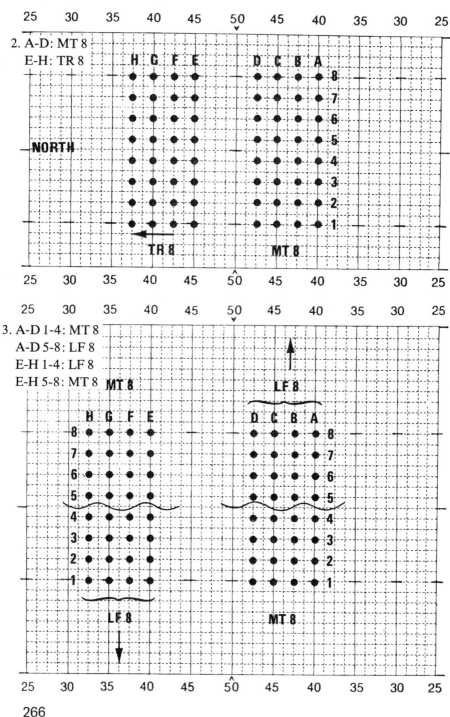

2. A-D: MT 8
   E-H: TR 8

3. A-D 1-4: MT 8
   A-D 5-8: LF 8
   E-H 1-4: LF 8
   E-H 5-8: MT 8

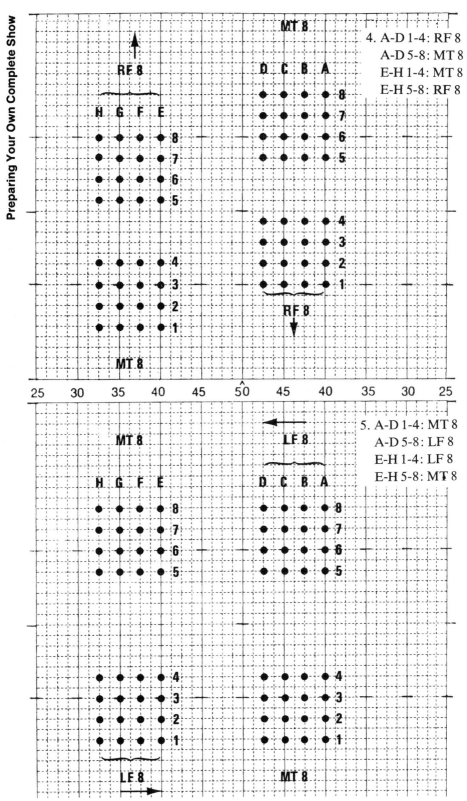

4. A-D 1-4: RF 8
   A-D 5-8: MT 8
   E-H 1-4: MT 8
   E-H 5-8: RF 8

5. A-D 1-4: MT 8
   A-D 5-8: LF 8
   E-H 1-4: LF 8
   E-H 5-8: MT 8

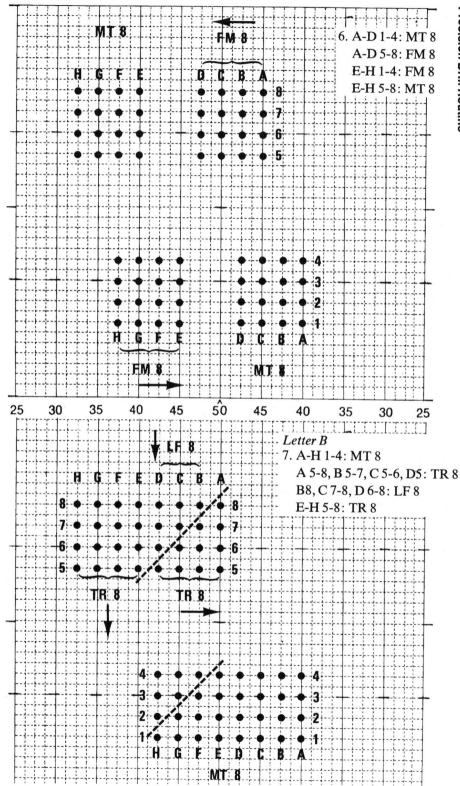

MT 8   FM 8

H G F E   D C B A

6. A-D 1-4: MT 8
   A-D 5-8: FM 8
   E-H 1-4: FM 8
   E-H 5-8: MT 8

8
7
6
5

H G F E   D C B A

4
3
2
1

FM 8   MT 8

25   30   35   40   45   50   45   40   35   30   25

LF 8

H G F E D C B A

8   8
7   7
6   6
5   5

TR 8   TR 8

Letter B
7. A-H 1-4: MT 8
   A 5-8, B 5-7, C 5-6, D5: TR 8
   B8, C 7-8, D 6-8: LF 8
   E-H 5-8: TR 8

4   4
3   3
2   2
1   1

H G F E D C B A

MT 8

268

8. A-D 1-4: TR 8
E 1-4, F 1-3, G 1-2, H1: LF 8
F4, G 3-4, H 2-4: TR 8
A-H 5-8: MT 8

9. All: FM 8

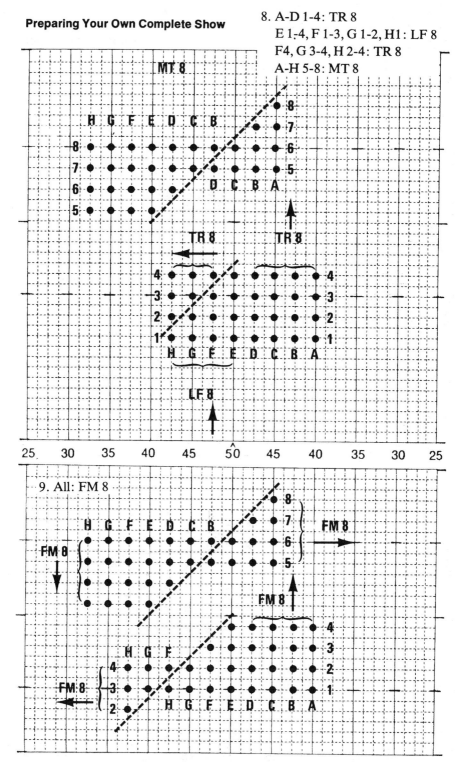

10. A-E 1-4, F 1-3, G 1-2, H1: TR 16
   A 5-8, B 5-7, C 5-6, D5: RF 16
   B8, C 7-8, D 6-8, E-H 5-8: LF 16
   F4, G 3-4, H 2-4: TR 16

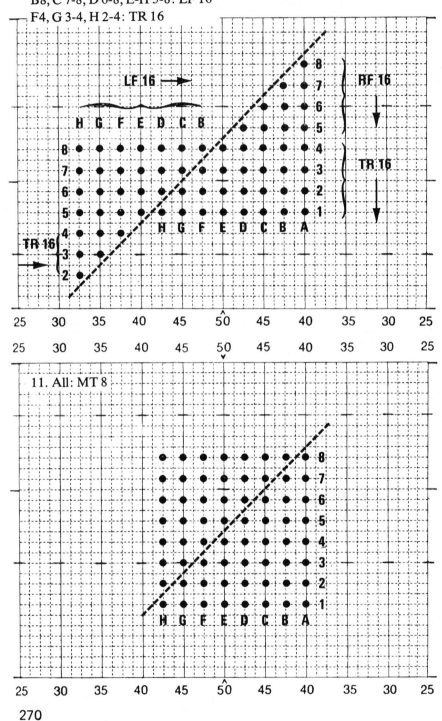

270

Preparing Your Own Complete Show

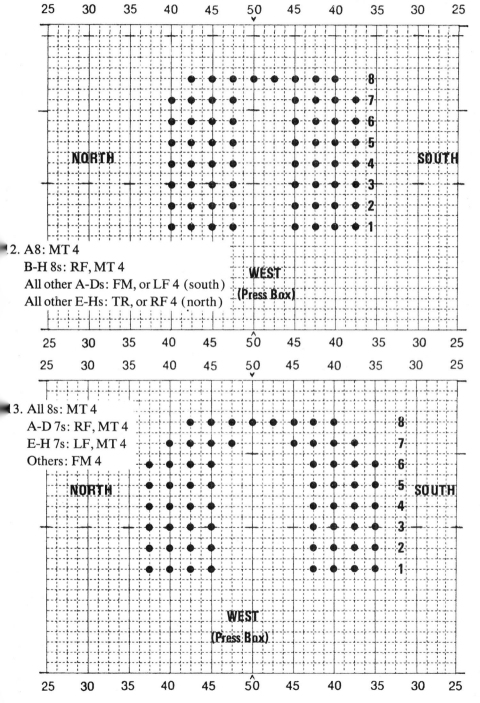

12. A8: MT 4
B-H 8s: RF, MT 4
All other A-Ds: FM, or LF 4 (south)
All other E-Hs: TR, or RF 4 (north)

WEST
(Press Box)

13. All 8s: MT 4
A-D 7s: RF, MT 4
E-H 7s: LF, MT 4
Others: FM 4

NORTH   SOUTH

WEST
(Press Box)

Precision Drill Routine

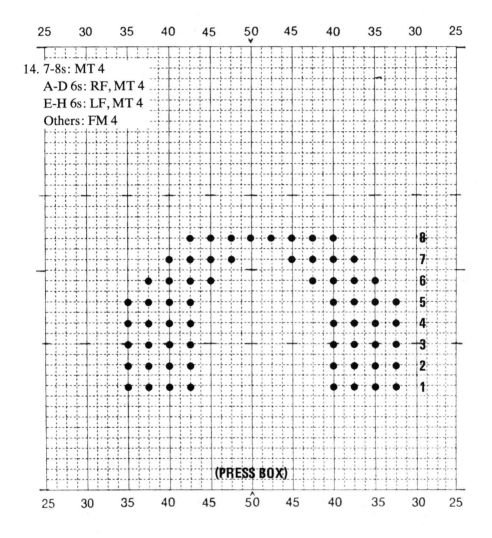

| 25 | 30 | 35 | 40 | 45 | 50 | 45 | 40 | 35 | 30 | 25 |

14. 7-8s: MT 4
    A-D 6s: RF, MT 4
    E-H 6s: LF, MT 4
    Others: FM 4

(PRESS BOX)

| 25 | 30 | 35 | 40 | 45 | 50 | 45 | 40 | 35 | 30 | 25 |

15. A-D 1-5s: RF, MT 4; H & C (Hit and Close)
    E-H 1-5s: LF, MT 4, H & C
    All others: MT 4; H & C

272

Sample solo cornet part:

Shoutin' Soul

Robert E. Foster

©Copyright MCMLXXIII by Alfred Publishing Co., Inc., New York

Concert Formation

You are now in a Concert Formation facing the press box, ready to play something to please the crowd and show off your band (like *The Screamer*). Stand fast and play!

Optional or Additional Formations

Optional or additional formations saluting or depicting a person, an object, or anything interesting or clever which is appropriate to the music, may be added at this point—between the concert formation and the final formation.

Final (School Salute) Formation

Music: *Boogie on Down* (see page 280).
Omit introduction, and begin at Letter A, standing in Concert Formation.

Letter A

1. All: Stand fast 4 measures (16 counts).
2.

A1-5: LF 4; MT 12	C8: LF 8; MT 8	F6: LF 4; MT 12
A6: LF 8; MT 8	D1-5: RF 8; MT 8	F7: MT 16
A7: LF 12; MT 4	D6: RF 4; MT 12	F8: RF 4; MT 12
A8: LF 16	D7: MT 16	G1-5: LF 4; MT 12
B1-5: MT 16	D8: LF 4; MT 12	G6: MT 16
B6: LF 4; MT 12	E1-5: LF 12; MT 4	G7: RF 4; MT 12
B7: LF 8; MT 8	E6: LF 8; MT 8	G8: RF 8: MT 8
B8: LF 12; MT 4	E7: LF 4; MT 12	H1-5: MT 16
C1-5: RF 4; MT 12	E8: MT 16	H6: RF 4; MT 12
C6: MT 16	F1-5: LF 8; MT 8	H7: RF 8; MT 8
C7: LF 4; MT 12		H8: RF 12; MT 4

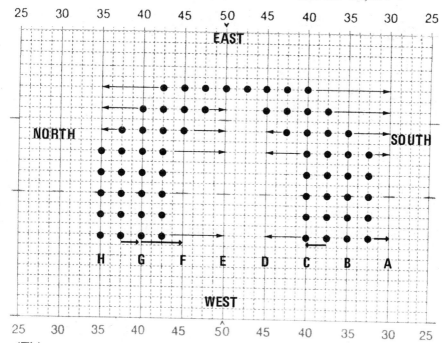

(This move returns each bandsman to his basic Rank position, but the Ranks are now five yards apart instead of two and a half).

274

3. All: Flank, or TR to face *East* 8 (returning to the center of the field); MT 8. (Do not play first ending. Go directly to second ending, and continue.)

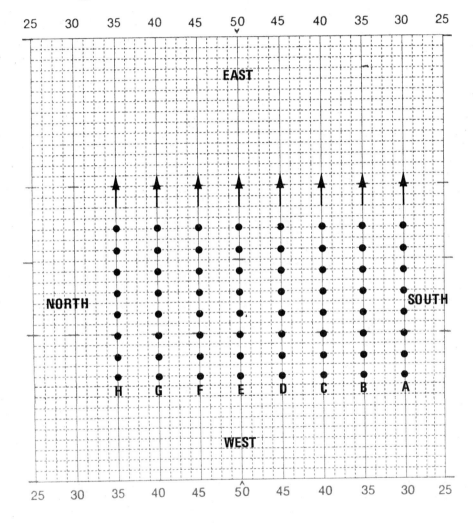

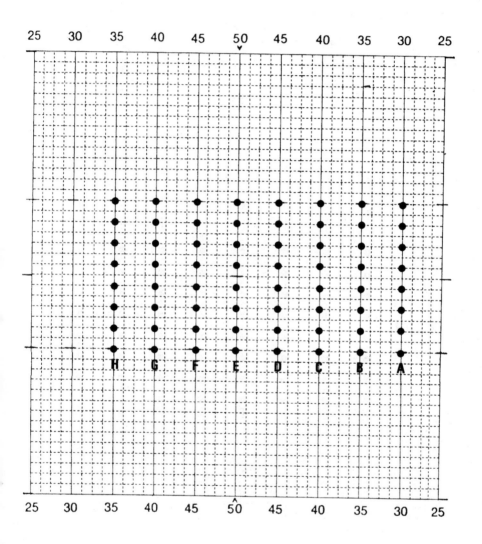

Letter B
4. Rank Leader's Drill to formation. When in correct position, face West and Mark Time until the end of the music. Hit and Close on first three beats of fifth measure from the end. (Repeat Letter B only if needed to provide more time.)

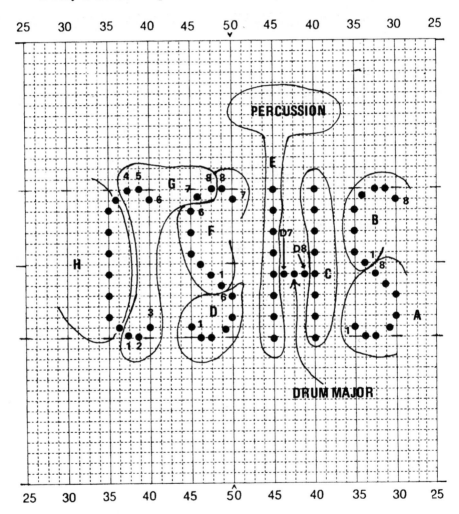

Sample solo cornet part

Boogie On Down

Exit

Start playing the most popular school fight song for your school, Marking Time and playing in place facing West Press Box and Home stands. At the beginning of the second time through, or at the beginning of the second half, do a To The Rear, and exit straight off the East sideline. This is simple, quick, and effective.

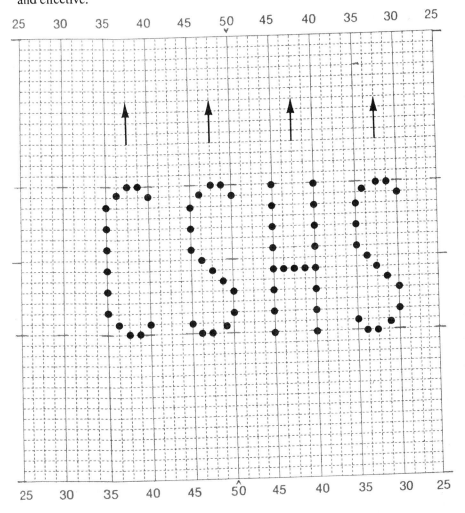

As band starts marching off the field, announcer says:

"AND THERE THEY GO, LADIES AND GENTLEMEN! THE COM-MACK SOUTH HIGH SCHOOL MARCHING RED DEVIL BAND!"